THE BALCONY

This Large Print Book carries the
Seal of Approval of N.A.V.H.

THE BALCONY

JANE DELURY

THORNDIKE PRESS
A part of Gale, a Cengage Company

Farmington Hills, Mich • San Francisco • New York • Waterville, Maine
Meriden, Conn • Mason, Ohio • Chicago

Thorndike Press, a part of Gale, a Cengage Company.

**LIBRARY OF CONGRESS CIP DATA ON FILE.
CATALOGUING IN PUBLICATION FOR THIS BOOK
IS AVAILABLE FROM THE LIBRARY OF CONGRESS**

ISBN-13: 978-1-4328-5579-6 (hardcover)

Published in 2018 by arrangement with Little, Brown and Company, a division of Hachette Book Group, Inc.

Printed in Mexico
1 2 3 4 5 6 7 22 21 20 19 18

For Cecilia Delury

CONTENTS

Au Pair. 9
Eclipse 57
A Place in the Country 76
Plunder 105
Nothing of Consequence 138
Half Life 158
The Pond. 194
Tintin in the Antilles 212
Ants 237
Between 262

ACKNOWLEDGMENTS 287

AU PAIR

In June of 1992, I left Boston for France with everything in front of me. For the next two months, I would be an au pair to Hugo and Olga Boyer's daughter, Élodie, at their country estate near Paris. The position came to me through my advisor at Boston University, where I'd just finished a master's degree in French and where Hugo would join the faculty in the fall. As Olga explained to my advisor, who asked me if I was interested, she and Hugo needed a *jeune fille* to help Élodie practice her English and to watch her mornings while Hugo worked on his book and Olga prepared the house for their departure. I would have a large, sunny room on the top floor and my afternoons and most of the weekends off. "Paris, with all of its delights, is only a brief train ride away," Olga wrote to me in French, her handwriting large and baroque. "Élodie is an easy child, and her father and I are not monsters." With the money I'd make, I could spend a third month in Paris and then see how I might stay on in France, where I believed I was meant to live.

When my advisor had mentioned a country estate, I imagined periwinkle shutters and roads lined with plane trees, fields of poppies and sunflowers, a village of church bells and cobblestone streets. Though I'd only been to Paris and to Nice, I thought I had an understanding of the French countryside, informed by the paintings of the impressionists and by novels such as *Madame Bovary*. The village of Benneville, however, turned out to be an industrial wash of smokestacks and faceless apartment buildings that ringed a center of ratty stucco storefronts. During the Second World War, Benneville had sat in the occupied zone, and the U.S. Air Force bombed the train station, missing their mark. The attack flattened the historic town center and shattered the church's stained-glass windows, now replaced by clear panes. There was the requisite monument to the wars, and the requisite square where pigeons pecked gravel around a fountain, and old people sat on benches, looking lonely. As for the Seine, that same river that glided through Paris under the Pont Mirabeau, inspiring poets and painters, looked sullen and stagnant in Benneville, the banks cluttered with factories.

The manor, as Olga referred to the house and grounds that composed the estate, was a five-minute drive from the village, protected from the surrounding ugliness by the pines and oaks of a *forêt domaniale.* Clearly, the house — a bourgeois *manoir* of buttery limestone that stretched three stories into slate turrets and gables — had once been magnificent, but it had been hastily and cheaply remodeled in the 1970s. Past the grand doors, the historic charm gave way to flocked wallpaper, chartreuse tile, and malachite linoleum. The questionable remodel hadn't been helped by Olga's predilection for knickknacks. A collection of ornate mantel clocks sat on the parlor shelves under a row of vintage perfume bottles. Ancient kitchen implements — a candle mold and *poissonnière,* a *moulin à légumes,* chalky with rust — cluttered the dining room walls.

"This is what happens when you lose everything to a war," Hugo told me as he carried my suitcase inside that first day. He skirted a stack of Turkish carpets rolled up like sausages.

"*Très drôle,*" Olga said. "I was a single

11

woman in an enormous house for years and years," she told me. "I needed to fill the space."

We climbed the marble waterfall of a staircase, Élodie's hand in mine. She was tiny for a four-year-old, with eyes the color of pennies and skin so pale that you could see a branch of veins on her right cheek. She'd adopted me instantly at the airport. On the drive to Benneville, she taught me the game of *barbichette.* She held my chin and I held hers, and the first one to laugh got a light slap on the cheek.

"Hugo and I are down that hall," Olga said on the second-floor landing, "with Élodie next door."

"I have a train set," Élodie said. "*Maman* set it up for me. It runs all the way under the bed." She squeezed my hand to punctuate her point.

Many of the ten bedrooms, Olga said as we went up the next flight, remained in the same *triste état,* or sad state, in which they'd been when she inherited the manor. "Thus all of the closed doors." She was determined, she said, to hold on to the house and the grounds, but the upkeep of a property like this one cost a fortune.

"If you hear thumping at night, don't fear ghosts," Hugo said. "It's only the pipes."

On the third floor, we walked into a room big as my entire apartment in Back Bay.

"*Et voilà,*" Olga said, "*votre petit coin de paradis.*"

French doors, open like most of the windows in the house, led to a balcony with a view of the forest. I could imagine a gilded dressing table and four-poster bed, although the current décor consisted of a vinyl armoire that closed with a zipper and a lumpy, high bed covered with a paisley duvet.

"It's the prettiest room," Olga said. "It was mine for years."

Hugo set down my bags. "*Vous n'êtes pas dépressive, j'espère.* We specifically requested a young woman in good mental health."

"Stop that, Hugo," Olga said. Once, she explained to me matter-of-factly, the lady of the house had jumped off the balcony, where Élodie had gone and was now calling to me to come join her. "Madame Léger had been in her youth a famous courtesan, a *grande horizontale* of the Second Empire. She was forty when she died. It was said that she hadn't taken well to the aging process."

"It might have only been meant as a dramatic gesture," Hugo said. "She had a *réputation de folle.* It is only three stories. Only she landed poorly and broke her neck."

"Don't worry," I said, as I went to join Élodie. "I grew up in the Midwest. We don't go crazy."

"Hemingway aside," Hugo said.

I had tried to be clever and he had out-clevered me. I was used to this kind of behavior from men in academia. I was a good student of French — solid in my verbal constructions, even the *plus-que-parfait,* versed in the gender distinctions of nouns. My accent was *passable.* My graduate school papers on Flaubert's love letters and the symbol of the corset in the nineteenth-century novel received As. But I was not brilliant. I would have preferred in some ways to be terrible.

Outside, Élodie stood on her tiptoes on the balcony, looking over the iron railing, which was supported by spindles that looped and twisted in a rusted web.

"Il y a un étang," Élodie said — there's a pond. She pointed at an island of light in the dark forest sprawling from the stone walls around the estate.

"We could walk to it."

She shook her head. "*On ne peut pas.* There are wolves."

Later, in the kitchen, as I helped Olga

make dinner, I asked her about what Élodie had said.

"Non," Olga said. "The wolves of France are long gone."

Élodie, she told me, had suffered a bad case of pneumonia that spring and had spent a week in the hospital. Her lungs remained weak, leaving her susceptible to another infection.

"We must not overexert her with long rambles. And the forest is filled with spores and damp." She was making a mayonnaise, whisking the egg yolk and oil in a bowl. "Élodie is stubborn," she said, "an adventuress, like you. We used to picnic by the pond. I told her that a villager had spotted a wolf. Sometimes you have to lie to children to keep them safe." She tilted the whisk in my direction. "Here, you try."

It was then, over the making of the mayonnaise, that I learned how my mornings with Élodie would go. There would be no borrowing the Renault to take her for ice cream at the *glacerie* I'd seen as we drove through Benneville, no excursions to nearby *lieux d'intérêt*. We would remain solely on the grounds of the estate. "Because I miss her, you see," Olga said, "though I have so much to do. I want to keep her close." She touched my elbow. "Try to go a bit faster. You want

15

the egg whites to conquer the oil or the mayonnaise won't take."

The next morning, I woke up to Olga's knock on the door and her voice calling, "*Il est huit heures,* Brigitte." I did a quick *toilette* in the adjoining bathroom, working my hair into a messy chignon and, since I was going to spend the morning with a four-year-old, putting on jeans and a T-shirt, which I'd ironed the previous night. These small details of domestic life — the ironing of everything, including sheets, the fact that milk was sold unrefrigerated and baking soda sold at the pharmacy, the smallness of toilet paper rolls, the gummy flaps of envelopes, the way Olga had asked me if I had my period because mayonnaise wouldn't set if made by a menstruating woman, the grains of sea salt in the butter we ate with the daily baguette — made that first week interesting. One afternoon, Olga took me with her to do the shopping, and we stood in front of the counter at the Boucherie Marcel as she and the butcher — an old man with a lip curled by a scar — explained to me the different cuts of meat: tripes and brains and blood sausages, the thick steaks of horse flank. I bought a copy of the newspaper *Libération* at the *tabac,* learned the names of politicians, drank my water without ice, perfected my chignon. I felt that I was becoming French, that the transformation begun in a middle school classroom years before was growing into a truth. I would learn, by living with Olga, and Hugo, and Élodie, a new authenticity.

Breakfast, we ate outside on a lopsided table in a cracked and mossy courtyard. Hugo finished before the rest of us, and then he'd retreat to his study for the duration of the day to work on his biography of the Malagasy poet Rado Koto. A specialist in the literature of the French colonies, Hugo had not seemed attractive in the book jacket photo I saw when I looked him up at the BU library — a middle-aged man with too much forehead and not enough chin, eccentric tufts of hair, and drooping eyes. In flesh and in bone, though, as the French goes, he let off the sensuality of the brilliant. He ran the Études Francophones department at the Sorbonne. His book on the literature of colonial Africa had made him a Knight of the Legion of Honor. According to grad student rumor at BU, he had approached the department about a position, and they'd created one for him. Several heads shorter than he, Olga was stout and pudgy-fingered, with graying hair that thinned around her temples, and a pair of reading glasses always on a chain around her neck. I'd calculated that she must be in her late forties, a few years older than Hugo. She had teased him once at dinner that he'd fallen in love with her because she kept the ink cartridges of his *stylos plumes* refilled, and I wouldn't have been surprised if this was true.

After Hugo had disappeared to his study, Olga would measure out Élodie's medicine drops into a glass of water and grenadine. Then Élodie and I took a collection of books from the still-unboxed library back outside, to a bench under a chestnut tree that was covered by fungal growths, as ribbed and full as outcrops of coral. We'd sit in the shade for an hour or two, the sun ticking over the forest. As I read aloud to Élodie, translated, and answered her questions, I was often elsewhere in my mind, planning a weekend trip to Paris, imagining the apartment I would find for my August in the city, and then — turning the pages, saying car, *voiture,* moon, *lune* — the great workings of my future: an under-the-table job in a bookstore or café, a student visa, enrollment in a PhD program, an apartment with a view of the Seine, lovers, a perfect accent, fresh croissants every morning from the bakery on the corner of my cobblestone street.

"*Regarde,* Brigitte," Élodie would say, looking up, "a bird."

"Don't move," I'd whisper, and Élodie would whisper, "No moving."

Above our heads, in the glossy canopy of chestnut leaves, a finch or sparrow rested on a branch, or worried a catkin with its beak.

"What does a bird say?" I'd ask after the bird flew away.

"Cheep, cheep," Élodie would say.

The differences between animal noises in French and English made Élodie laugh. Why did a bird say cheep, cheep in English and *cui, cui* in French? Why did one pig oink and another pig *groin, groin*? Why woof, woof instead of *ouaf, ouaf*? Did a rooster that cried cock-a-doodle-doo know to cry *cocorico* instead if it moved to France? "Do rivers sound different in America too, Brigitte?" she asked me once.

Done reading, we'd take the path cut into a jungle of ivy and weeds back to the courtyard and leave the books on the breakfast table. Élodie would call out, *"Maman,"* once, twice, to the rear of the manor until Olga appeared from this window or that, like the cuckoo in the clock. "We are going for our walk now," Élodie added, in English, as I'd taught her, and Olga would wave and tell us, in French, to have a good time and to be safe, as if we were heading off into the forest or along the road to Benneville, when in fact our walk would only take us around the manor and down the front drive.

The first night at dinner, Olga had told me the history of the property and of the surrounding area. Benneville had never been *une métropole,* she said, even before the destruction of the war. The village got its name from a monk on pilgrimage to the tomb of Saint Denis in Paris who, having stopped by the Seine for the night, cured a child of smallpox with his blessing. Over the centuries, the land around the village had been forested and used as hunting grounds for the royal party as an alternative to Fontainebleau. After the revolution, fields replaced forest. The commerce on the Seine moved to bigger ports such as Honfleur, and people mostly made a living through sustenance farming. One such farming family produced a boy named Jean-Paul Léger, who joined the French army, fought in the Second Opium War, and, having learned the secrets of silkworm farming, opened a factory in Lyon and became the leading supplier of silk to the regime of the Second

Empire. When Léger made his first fortune, he bought a large parcel of the forest where he'd played as a child to build a summer estate for his wife and son. Limestone from a quarry that later became the pond gave the façade its luminescent exterior. The walls of the manor were papered in silk from the Léger factory, and the ironwork of the balcony and of a pergola in the garden was designed to resemble silk thread. In addition to the manor, there was a cottage near the main road to house the estate's servants.

Léger's son, who inherited the property, had no children, his wife, the aforementioned *grande horizontale,* having broken her neck on the flagstones of the courtyard. The manor was "never quite so grand again," Olga said. The next owner, an *industriel* named Émile Vouette, expanded the only real commerce in Benneville at the time, a sawmill on the Seine that had been converted into a nightclub. "You might have noticed the blinking breasts on the roof from the *nationale,*" Olga said. After Émile Vouette died, his widow eventually sold the former servants' cottage and grew old alone in the manor. Her son, in turn, sold the property to Olga's parents in 1943.

"They had tried to immigrate to the U.S. and were denied visas," Olga said. "So they came here. I suppose they thought they'd be safe this far from the city. They had forged identity cards and millions of francs in cash. But they were arrested by the Gestapo soon after they moved into the manor and were sent to Drancy."

Olga's mother was pregnant at the time of the arrest, and Olga was born in the camp. A worker, later hanged by the French *milice,* smuggled the baby to safety in a laundry cart. Olga was raised in an orphanage in Paris. After some legal battles, the property came to her as the legal owner. The manor had been destroyed by looters during the war, Olga's parents' belongings sold on the black market. "Nothing remained," she told me, except for a set of wooden nesting dolls — the outside figure an old woman in a red and yellow sarafan — that stood on Élodie's nightstand. The dolls, Olga said, were originals from Abramtsevo, near Moscow, where her parents had lived before moving to France. "Someone must have put them back."

Olga had repaired and remodeled the interior of the manor as best she could. Later, she met Hugo at the Sorbonne, where she worked as a librarian, and once they were married, moved to his apartment on the rue Mouffetard, my favorite street in

Paris. Summers, they spent in Benneville. "Hugo gets bored out here in the country," Olga had said. "But it's good for his focus. We don't socialize. We are considered summer people, and I remain a Jew."

Having exchanged our goodbyes with Olga, Élodie and I headed along the courtyard, past a dry marble fountain shaped like an urn and circled by the pedestals of missing statues. We snaked through the maze of an overgrown topiary — where Élodie stopped to name the shapes she saw in the messy bushes (a cat, a dog, a castle), then passed by a muddle of vines and nettles that humped over horned and shriveled rosebushes. In the middle of the rose garden was the iron pergola, the design of which matched the balcony and which had been meant, originally, to resemble a cocoon. Now, dripping with ivy and ropes of wisteria, it looked instead like a sea monster, tentacles reaching every which way.

At the front of the manor, we continued on toward the main road, hopping over the shadows of the plane trees that lined the drive. I made up stories that involved princesses, ogres, witches, and goblins. If the plot got too quiet — a princess locked in her tower too long, waiting for a prince — Élodie would prompt me. *"Et donc,"* she'd say, and I'd add in a knock at the door, a sudden storm, the hand of a giant raised to the window, offering escape.

Where the drive met the main road, we turned around to go back to the manor, passing, again, the former servants' cottage: a tight two-story house made of meaner stone than the manor, with a lichen-blotched roof and a lopsided chimney. The lawn in front ran to the road, broken up by beds of peonies. Out back, a well, closed with a sheet of metal, stood near a massive vegetable garden with a fence draped in raspberry vines. An old man and his wife, Monsieur and Madame Havre, lived in the cottage. During the war, Olga had told me, Monsieur Havre was the director of the boys' school in Benneville and a leader of the local resistance. Now he was as slow and stiff as an automaton, often outside, hunched over a row of beans or training cucumber vines in the vegetable garden.

By the second week of this calm routine, I was well over my jet lag and starting to feel stir crazy. Would they mind, I asked Hugo and Olga at breakfast, if I used the bicycle that I'd seen in the potting shed behind the pergola? I thought I'd go for a ride on one of the logging roads that cut through the forest.

"What bicycle?" Hugo said. He was dunking a piece of baguette into his bowl of coffee as Olga cut toast into strips for Élodie to dip in the yolk of her soft-boiled egg.

"Mine," Olga said. She cracked the crown of the egg with a spoon. "It must be terribly rusted now."

"I didn't notice," I said.

"Oh, to have the eyes of the young," Hugo said. He looked over at Olga. "I didn't know you could ride a bicycle."

"I used to take it to the village for bread, before the road became a *nationale*," she said, scooping the egg off the shell. "Now you'd risk your life."

That afternoon, Élodie down for her nap, Olga helped me to clean the cobwebs from the bike, fill the tires with air, and drip oil on the chain. I headed off shakily over the blanket of grass and ivy to the gate that led to the forest. My father had taught me to ride a bike in the driveway of our rancher in the suburbs of Chicago, one hand on the back of the banana seat and another on my shoulder. Like other suburban kids in the 1970s, I rode without a helmet or supervision to the bowling alley and shopping mall. Chicago was flat, and it wasn't until I was older, doing my undergraduate studies at UC Berkeley, that I discovered mountain biking and the excitement of hills. This bike, though, was the furthest you could imagine from a mountain bike, with narrow tires, a high frame, and no suspension. Still, it could go fast. By my second outing, I knew the trails that forked into thicker paths that forked into logging roads. I cranked the pedals, whipped around turns, braced myself when the front tire hit a rut or a tree root, maneuvered around the pyramids of felled logs.

On my fourth ride, near a clearing wild with daisies, I found the pond Élodie had shown me from the balcony, the former stone quarry. It was about half the size of a football field with banks cut at jig-jag angles. On one side, willow trees spilled in a fluorescent blur. On the other side was a heap of quarried stone of the same creamy color as the manor, topped by a marble cross. Water lilies floated on the surface of the pond, dragonflies hovering, butterflies flitting, the willow trees shushing. The quiet was beautiful. I laid down the bike and, in one of those moments of youthful solitude when one is one's own voyeur, took off my shorts and T-shirt and slipped down the bank. I dog-paddled between the water lilies until I noticed that my arms were coated in a layer of slime. The quiet suddenly felt foreboding. I swam back toward the shore. Maybe, I thought, during the German occupation, the bodies of partisans had been thrown into the quarry, thus the cross. Maybe I was floating in a burial ground. I swam faster, pulled myself up the bank, panicky now, then put on my clothes and rode back quickly to the manor, where I showered the slime from my skin.

A week or so into my riding, I came out of the forest to find Hugo standing with Élodie near the rose garden, looking down at the grass, a cigarette between his thumb and middle finger.

"A toad," Élodie said. "We're going to catch it."

"We're trying to, anyway," Hugo told me. "She woke up early from her nap. And Olga is at the butcher's, pursuing a roast."

"I can take over if you need to work," I said.

"No. I'm stuck anyway. I'm writing with no idea of where I'm going. Pedaling with my eyes closed, as you seem to do." He smiled. "You go fast on that old thing. I wouldn't want to be on a trail when you come by."

"I like to go fast," I said.

Through the cigarette smoke, I smelled alcohol, that smell it takes on in a man when he's had a lot to drink and it's evaporating through the pores of his skin. I understood now why a bottle of mineral water accompanied our dinners rather than a bottle of wine, understood the lack of the traditional aperitif.

"It's a baby." Élodie dropped to her hands and knees to study the toad.

"Or maybe it's a frog," I said.

As the three of us approached the toad, it jumped between my legs.

Hugo tossed aside the cigarette. "I'll get you, you little sneak." He lunged at the toad and plucked it from the grass. *"Victoire."* He looked at me as the toad writhed and batted its feet. "What have I been doing inside that house when there were delights like this right outside?"

"Let it go, Papa." Élodie said. "Please. It doesn't like that. I don't want to catch it anymore."

Hugo set the toad in the grass and it hopped away. He leaned over to kiss Élodie on the top of her head.

"You're right, *ma bichette,*" he said. *"Pardonne-moi."*

Élodie's face looked thin and tight. I was afraid she would cry. "Let's make crêpes, shall we?" I said. Olga had shown me how to mix the thin batter, and Élodie laughed at my attempts at flipping the crêpes into the air and catching them in the pan.

"We will never have her goodness," Hugo said as we followed Élodie back to the house. He looked chagrined. And he was definitely tipsy.

"I certainly won't," I said.

Élodie chattered away ahead of us, and we weren't listening. Hugo pointed at the fountain. "Nine pedestals," he said. "You know what that must mean."

I hadn't seen this detail before. *"Les Muses?"*

"Gone," he said. "Every last one of them. I'll have to find my inspiration elsewhere." He smiled at me again. "I'll tell you a secret. I don't know how to ride a bicycle."

"I could teach you."

"I'm sure you could," he said.

That was when things shifted. I'd become more interesting to Hugo as I flew out of the forest into his alcohol daze, and he became more interesting to me. He was an obsessive genius with an addiction. He was smart and tortured. I'd discovered his allure.

At dinner that night, he asked if I'd heard of the Malagasy poet Rado Koto, the subject of his book. Well, I said, I'd read some of Koto's poems in an anthology when my advisor told me about Hugo's research. "In case you asked me that question."

"Perhaps I was waiting for you to ask," he said.

The four of us were eating *bœuf bourguignon* at a dining room table stacked with dishes waiting to be boxed.

"Did you read his poem 'Benneville'?" Hugo asked. "It's about the village."

If I had, I said, I didn't remember. Hugo went to his study for Koto's first book, which had won the Prix Guillaume Apollinaire and had been translated by the American poet John Ashbery to great acclaim in the U.S. Like most French books, this one was of simple design, without author photo or biography. In "Benneville," a woman returns to her "village of ashes," and walks, barefoot, down "streets still snowing black." She leaves having found nothing, "not even the memory of what she sought."

"Tell it to me, Brigitte," Élodie said. She'd come around to the back of my chair.

"*C'est pour les grands,* Élodie," Olga told her, and brought her gently back to her lap. Her overprotectiveness irritated me more and more.

"Did he live here?" I asked Hugo.

"No," Hugo said. To his knowledge Koto had never even seen the village. He wrote the poem before he'd stepped foot in France. He'd been living in Antananarivo, Madagascar's capital, making his living as a tutor and writing poems in an apartment without electricity or running water. "I suppose he read about Benneville's destruction or someone told him about it."

"It's beautiful," I said, wishing I had something deeper to add.

"Beautiful poems, maybe," Olga said, "but a miserable, short life."

Koto, she said, had become addicted to heroin, "and then," she whispered over Élodie's head, "a belt and a chandelier in a room at the Ritz. And he was so young. Such a waste."

"What Koto did not have was the love of a woman like you, *ma chérie,*" Hugo said. Koto, he told me, had been at the height of his creative powers when he succumbed to addiction — "forty-two, which I suppose to you seems ancient." The very boundaries of Malagasy culture that Koto protested in his later poems, written once he'd moved to Paris — taboos, ritual, pagan worship — had nonetheless provided him with a girding he'd lost when he immigrated to France and found what he called in one poem "messy liberty."

"He had an affair with your Andy Warhol," Olga said. "It ended badly."

"Olga is not a romantic," Hugo said. "For instance, she refutes the theory that this estate is cursed."

She didn't like to talk about it, he continued, but it was not only Madame Léger who had died tragically. One of the other inhabitants had drowned in the pond, thus the cross on the bank. "Who was it, again?" he asked Olga.

"Not in front of Élodie," Olga said. She shook her head. "I don't believe in curses. I believe that life is difficult and that people can be stupid and cruel." She went back to cutting Élodie's meat.

Although I didn't believe in curses either, I believed that a place could feel cursed. I was fourteen when my father's heart stopped while he was walking the dog in our neighborhood. "Must be a fire," my mother said of the sirens we heard from the backyard. Then the dog showed up at the fence, trailing its leash. That was the end of my childhood, and the beginning of my wanting to leave. I'd never much liked my landscape of tract housing and mini-malls. After my father died, that landscape became sinister.

"Olga talks around things," Hugo said. "I shall confess to you as well. I fear that I

32

strayed this afternoon in my pledge of sobriety. Olga found me out immediately. She has the nose of a mouse."

"Tomorrow is another day," Olga said. "Isn't that the American expression?"

I nodded and kept my face blank, feeling that I was trespassing on their intimacy, and also feeling culpable. That afternoon, before I came across him and Élodie on the lawn, Hugo had driven to the café and had a beer or a glass of wine, probably several. This he'd revealed to Olga. That afternoon, too, he had taken me in as I rode out of the woods, opened his gaze to me, said I could teach him to ride a bike. This he'd kept between us.

In mid-July, I went to Paris for a weekend. I sat in Les Deux Magots, taking notes in a journal with the plume pen I'd bought at a *papeterie*. At a table by the window, I changed my signature, which I found too looping and girlish. I wrote my name over and over on a page until the letters shrank, tightened, became almost unintelligible. I walked the Marais, where I wanted to live, drank mint tea in the mosque of Paris, and bought *macarons* at Ladurée. At Shakespeare and Company, I left my CV with George Whitman, the store's celebrated founder, who offered to put me up when I returned at the end of the summer. On the terrace of a café, standing in the pastel haze of Monet's water lilies at the Jeu de Paume, mounting the steps of Sacré Cœur, I felt the gaze of men drift over me and linger. I'd had sex for the first time at eighteen with my high school boyfriend, and two partners since: with condoms and in the missionary position. My masturbatory fantasy life, however, was rich and varied, my imaginary lovers bold and adventurous. William Hurt in *Body Heat*. Richard Gere in *American Gigolo*. Of late, when I came, I thought about Hugo.

At the Benneville train station, Olga waited on the quays in a shapeless dress and closed-toe sandals, shadows under her eyes. She asked where I'd gone in Paris and what I'd eaten. "I won't miss the city," she said. "It was too noisy and crowded and dirty. *Cependant,*" she added, as we walked to the car, for a girl like me, there was nothing like the capital. "Élodie wanted to come fetch you," she said, "but she's had a cough so I left her at the cottage with Madame Havre." She was glad I was back, she said, because she still needed to finish the third floor of the manor before they left, and Hugo was *"bloqué"* with his book. He was at a conference in Pau for several days.

At the cottage, Élodie came to the door with Madame Havre, the wife of the man in the vegetable garden, a woman in a house-dress and apron with thick ankles and swollen knuckles. Élodie hugged my waist and said she'd missed me. "I thought you'd never return."

"Was she all right?" Olga asked, and Madame Havre said *oui*, Élodie hadn't coughed once, and they'd played two games of peg solitaire.

"The marbles come from Africa," Élodie said.

"My sons used to love that game," Madame Havre said, so much, in fact, that the youngest had tried to eat one of the marbles. Her grandsons were visiting *en ce moment*, she added, and she'd convinced them to play too. *"Ils sont gentils avec leur vieille peau de grand-mère,"* she said — they are kind to their old grandmother. She called down the hall and a dreadlocked teenager waved to us vaguely from a doorway without lifting the earphones of his Walkman off his head.

"Why don't the two of you go read in the library?" Olga said when we were back in the manor. "Élodie needs a quiet afternoon to get over that cough."

Sometimes I wondered if Olga had

Munchausen syndrome by proxy. Élodie's cough was light and infrequent, the kind you might have with allergies. But then, I told myself, Olga must be anxious. She was about to leave her country, and her husband was at a conference most likely on a bender, maybe even sleeping around.

He called that night after dinner. I heard the ripples of Olga's voice from the parlor, where I sat reading next to a fan. The manor had been hot before I left. Now it felt muggy and musty. One wall of the parlor had a huge fireplace made from the same stone as the manor and carved with butterflies and bunches of grapes. I could hear an animal scurrying around in the chimney and hoped it was a squirrel, not a rat. Down the hall, Olga sat at a secretary, speaking into a hulking phone that seemed to date from the 1950s. Her voice rose. The receiver clunked down. Instead of going up the stairs, she came into the parlor. She sat down on the couch and reached into the pocket of her robe.

"Would you smoke this with me?" she said. "I bought it from Madame Havre's grandson. He supplies me occasionally."

It seemed miraculous, that joint in her hand, like the pumpkin becoming a carriage.

"Avec plaisir," I said.

"I've never been a drinker, though I liked a glass of wine with dinner. I stopped completely for Hugo. I only do this sometimes."

We passed the joint between us. She held it as Hugo held his cigarettes, between her thumb and middle finger.

"Hugo slurred my name on the phone," she said. "It isn't that hard to say, is it?"

"Olga." I pronounced it slowly, already stoned. The lights had blurred and the cardboard boxes by the door bobbled. Olga curled into a corner of the couch, knees tucked under her arms. "Hugo won't remember that conversation tomorrow," she said. "He blacks out. He can lose an afternoon or an evening like that." She snapped her fingers, soundlessly. "When I met him, he was writing his biography of Jacques Roumain. He'd sit at a desk in the library surrounded by books, ripping pieces of paper to mark chapters, and some of them would fall to the floor." I offered her the joint. *"Il était tellement concentré,"* she said after taking another hit. "But his hands shook. I thought he had palsy. *Eh ben, non.* It was withdrawal. He was trying to stop drinking on his own. We started to date. We'd go to the cinema, have dinner. He said he found me refreshing. He'd always been with emotional, unsteady women like the one who jumped from the balcony of your room."

She wanted to save him, she told me, and she wanted a child. She was already in her forties, and the chances seemed close to none. The summer after they met, she got pregnant. They came to the estate and Hugo started his research on Koto.

"He took meeting me as a sign that he should write this book," Olga said. "What were the chances that a scholar of franco-phone literature should end up with a woman from a town immortalized by one of Madagascar's greatest poets?" She laughed. "I can see from your face that you are skeptical. Yet I'm sure you know about the meanings one makes when first in love. Coincidences become destiny." Her eyes seemed darker, her face longer, more myste-rious. As she let out a sigh of smoke, I saw what Hugo might have found in her, at least when they first met. "Beginning the book was difficult for him," she said, "and so is the middle, and so will be the end. The fact that he's drinking again so much is not surprising. But we have Élodie now. And we must do our best for her."

"*Ça va aller,*" I said. If there was a better

expression than "It will be all right," I didn't know it.

I thought, maybe, that this evening meant that Olga would loosen up about everything, including Élodie. She didn't. The next morning, she said Élodie had been up twice during the night with the cough, so we should stay inside again. She'd taken Élodie to the doctor while I was in Paris, and in addition to the morning drops for her weak lungs, there were new drops in her evening chocolate, vitamin tablets to chew, and a blood sausage as an afternoon snack to give her more iron.

For the next few days, Olga went up and down the stairs with boxes, while I sat on the floor of Élodie's room hooking train tracks under the bed for the new routes she designed. I taught her how to make a cat's cradle with a piece of twine. We colored and drew. We read books in the library. "Tell me a story," she would say, her head on my lap. Outside, the expanse of the grounds and the forest, the ability to move, had made me imaginative. Here, in the dim library, my mind shrank. I disappointed Élodie, I'm sure, with my stories, but she never let on.

Hugo came back from the conference with stubble on his cheeks and lavender sachets for Olga and me. Olga sniffed hers and said,

"One more thing to pack."

"Don't be cross," he said. "I had to go."

Élodie sat on his lap playing with her present, a cicada made of tin that whirred its wings when you pressed a button on its back.

"The more sun they get, the louder they sing," Hugo told her.

"Mistral," I said.

"The wind?" Olga asked.

"The poet," Hugo said.

"Il veut voler," Élodie said.

"We'll help him, then." Hugo pinched the cicada between his fingers and swooped it up and down, past Élodie's ear, over her head, then over mine, making her laugh. I saw that Olga was observing me.

Over the next week, Hugo was in his study before breakfast, and he ate his dinner there on a tray. I'd see him at the window when I came back from my bike rides, which I stretched across the afternoons. I picked daisies and buttercups for Élodie and we wove flower chains at the kitchen table. Mostly, I wanted our time together to move faster. Meanwhile, Olga rolled up rugs, sorted clothes, wrapped frames and knick-knacks in newspaper. She finished the library. Her organizing and packing had a faster pace. The renters would come for the keys at the end of the month, and then the Boyers would be off to Boston.

One morning, I woke up early and came downstairs, feeling sweaty and grumpy. During the night, I'd stripped off my clothes, run a towel under cold water, and plastered it on my body to cool down. I missed air conditioning.

"You're awake," Hugo said from the doorway of his study. He was dressed as he'd been the night before, his shirt unbuttoned so his chest hair showed.

"I was hot," I said.

He wobbled. He'd been drinking. "This is nothing. Try Tunisia in summer. Come, would you?"

I'd never been in his study. Columns of books stood all over the floor, and jam jars filled with fountain pens lined a shelf. "I use a different one each day," Hugo said of the pens. "It keeps the thoughts fresh, or used to." He pointed at the pages of his book manuscript, open on the desk. The paper glowed with the colors of the rainbow, spilling over the tight march of Hugo's handwriting.

I held my hand over the paper. My palm turned scarlet. "How?" I said.

"Look more carefully."

I felt the distance between our bodies.

41

Turning around, I saw a bottle of rum on the windowsill. A beam of sunlight trapped inside projected a prism onto the desk. "It's mocking my words with its beauty," Hugo said. "I think I'll have to quit for the day."

"You could also move the bottle off the windowsill," I said. I meant to tease him, but the words came out hard, not coy.

Hugo laughed softly and went back to the chair behind his desk. *"Tu es si américaine,"* he said.

Two weeks later, he was no longer trying to hide his drinking. He'd be at breakfast, holding Élodie on his lap, teasing Olga, dunking his croissant into his coffee, and in the afternoon, the car would be gone to the café. Olga dealt with it as you would deal with a child. One night, at dinner, Hugo fell asleep at the table, and she shook him awake, gently, then helped him upstairs.

"What is wrong with Papa?" Élodie asked when Olga came back.

"Papa is playing," Olga said.

The spell between Hugo and me felt broken by that moment in his study. Now I noticed his untucked shirts, his crooked bottom teeth, the ridged surface of his nails. And as if he knew that he'd shown me too much of his weakness, he no longer tried to flirt or smiled at me in the same way.

A week before I left for Paris for good, when I returned from my bike ride, he came again to the doorway of his study.

"You're bleeding," he said.

"I hit a tree."

I was out of breath and still shaky. I'd rounded a turn by the pond and misjudged the space between two trunks. I'd gone over the top of the bike and scraped my cheek on a tree root. Hugo leaned toward me. I thought he would kiss me. Instead, he folded me in his arms. He smelled sour and sad. I made myself stay until he released me.

"Olga will take care of that wound," he said. *Elle répare tout.*

In the bathroom upstairs, Olga dabbed a cotton pad of disinfectant on my cheek. Élodie's cough had cleared, but the evening before she'd developed a fever, and Olga said she'd been up with her all night.

"I'll take her to her doctor in Paris today," she said, her eyes bleary and steady. "We'll stay the night. I won't mind if something happens with Hugo while I'm away."

At first, I thought I'd misunderstood, then I took a step back. "How can you say that?"

She looked up at me with that face I thought so plain and doughy.

"I'd rather he do that than drink."

43

"Je ne suis pas une pute," I said.

"I'm not saying you are." She shrugged. "I see how Hugo looks at you, and I see how you look at him. I am only telling you that it is all right if you want to."

"I don't. And I thought you loved him."

She smiled at me, wearily. "Silly girl," she said. "What can you possibly know about love?"

At breakfast the next morning, Olga, Hugo, and I pretended that nothing had happened. Olga left with Élodie for Paris and Hugo shut himself in his study. After riding the bike to Benneville along the buzzing *nationale,* I spent the afternoon reading at a café. I ate an early dinner at a pizzeria on the square and rode back to the manor at dusk to find the house empty and Hugo's car gone. The next day, and for the rest of the week once Olga and Élodie returned, the three of us ignored one another as best we could. We lavished attention on Élodie, played word games with her at dinner, smiled at her as she drew at the table with her pencil set. If I'd been relieved to leave for Paris once before, I was even more so the day I returned the bike to the potting shed for the last time, and packed my bags. I never wanted to see that forest or that house again.

In front of the manor, I kissed Élodie and Hugo on the cheeks, and then Olga drove me to the train station.

"Bon . . ." she said as we stood on the quays, an expression that can be translated as "Well, then," and which means "There is nothing more to say." *"Merci pour tout,"* I said. I didn't kiss her goodbye. The train doors opened. It all felt, I thought by the time I reached Paris, very French, very European, like something in a film by Godard.

I took George Whitman of Shakespeare and Company up on his offer and for the next month was a Tumbleweed, one of a group of young expatriates who lived and worked at the store. I slept in the bed with velvet drapes near the children's section. I read the required book a day, and wrote in my notebook, fragments I thought well tuned and compelling. By the time the linden trees along the Seine had rusted, I'd enrolled at the University of Paris and found an apartment — a former maid's room — in the fourteenth arrondissement. On New Year's Eve, at a discothèque, I danced to ABBA with the man who would become my husband. After two years of romance and sex and long conversations on his *clic-clac,* I moved into his larger apartment in a building with peeling shutters and a rackety elevator that I found charming. He finished his PhD in literature and started to teach. I took the CAPES and found a position at a high school. I wrote and abandoned two chapters of a novel. I tried poetry instead, and mailed my first efforts abroad to literary journals, hoping that the foreign stamps would help my chances. The first baby came.

Sometimes, in those early years of marriage, I'd regret my answer to Olga. What harm would it have done if I'd slept with Hugo? It would have been the last wild act of my life before I fell in love and committed to monogamy. Should I have been so offended by Olga's proposition? And what had offended me, really? She'd been onto me, to my attempts at banter with Hugo, to the way I tilted my head toward him, to my desire to be desired. She was smarter than I thought. Sometimes, when my husband and I made love, I'd imagine he was Hugo. It was a fantasy that returned more often after our second child was born.

One afternoon when my younger child was three, I ran into my advisor from Boston University while waiting for my husband in front of his office. My advisor was at the university for a conference. He said he'd wondered what had happened to me. I told the story that already was starting to feel like fiction — how after that summer in Benneville I hadn't wanted to go back to the United States and so I stayed on in France and then met my husband, how wonderful it was to live in Paris, how I liked teaching at the lycée, how I had published a few poems in journals he would never have heard of, although he said that he had.

"I meant to apologize to you," he said. "I always felt that I had a part in the Boyers' plan even though I was in the dark when I suggested the position to you."

I said I didn't know what he was talking about, so he told me. The department at BU had been surprised when Hugo and Olga arrived in Boston that August of 1992 and Élodie immediately started treatments for leukemia at Children's Hospital. Élodie, he said, was only in the beginning stages of the disease. When she had been diagnosed in Paris the previous spring, Olga did research and learned about a new treatment with minimal side effects and good outcomes offered in several American hospitals. Hugo approached French literature departments in those cities.

Olga and Élodie used to come by the

department offices, he said, and, aside from Élodie's baldness, you wouldn't think that she was ill.

"She was such a happy child, as you must know," my advisor said.

The treatments were successful and the cancer in remission by the following year. Hugo, though, fell apart. His drinking worsened. He came to class incoherent. "He never finished the book on Koto." After a few years, the department had let him go, but my advisor helped him to find a position at Syracuse, "a real step down, with a bad teaching load."

"I had no idea that she was so sick," I said, although already I saw that I had, saw all of the clues I'd ignored because my attention was elsewhere.

"They wouldn't have wanted you to know, either, I suppose," my advisor said, "since you might tell me. Olga told me later that they wanted to get to Boston and secure health insurance. She feared the arrangement could fall through."

My husband came out of his office after my advisor had left. I didn't tell him about that conversation. I remember, distinctly, inhabiting the moment in that smoky hallway when I could tell him or not tell him, and choosing not to. I kept it to myself, along with glances exchanged on the street, a walk alone on the quays of the Seine, a concert in the Sainte-Chapelle that I slipped into alone. I was practicing the art of deception that I would need to have an affair.

When I look back now, it was a simple story, a crude and common one. But at the time, every moment of my day shimmered. I was returning home from school on the Metro, a sack of student papers between my ankles, when the man next to me asked my name. He said he'd seen me before on this train. He was a cartoonist for a political magazine with a name everyone now knows. He told me I seemed sad. *Tu as l'air triste,* he said. "Here, I'll show you."

There is probably a joke about a cartoonist picking up a woman on a train, but I found the drawing beautiful. In a few lines, he showed me to myself: I was someone pensive and deep and experienced, someone with so much she wanted to say that her mouth bowed. Later, he told me that talking to me that day was the boldest act of his life. He said that if I hadn't stared at him directly in the eyes, he never would have. I have no memory of having done so, and that doesn't sound like the woman I was when I boarded the train that afternoon, although another woman walked off with that torn-out drawing in the pocket of her raincoat, a phone number scribbled on the back.

It lasted a year. I'm aghast when I look back at myself: sitting at the breakfast table stirring the children's hot chocolate, talking to my husband about taking the car in for service, and then, a few hours later, lying on a hotel bed with my legs spread wide. What I did was wrong. Unforgivable. Sometimes, though, I think that I will never feel as alive as I did during those months of wickedness. Suddenly I didn't know who I was, and it was exhilarating. I became, at forty-two, that girl again, in a city, not a forest, on foot, rather than on a bicycle. I was twenty years older than she was and just as naïve and reckless and unthinking. Anything seemed possible. A single life could split into many. Who knew what the future held? An apartment over a river? Trips to countries I'd never seen? What we were doing was impossible; still, maybe, just maybe, we would end up together.

One afternoon, I was on the sofa, grading papers, the television murmuring on low volume when a special broadcast announced the attacks at *Charlie Hebdo*. I felt the same terror I'd felt when the dog showed up without my father. I had no one to call. I didn't know if he was in the office — we knew each other's days only vaguely, not as you know the days of your spouse. I paced the apartment, from the children's bedroom to the kitchen, telling myself to stay calm, watching the news, turning on the radio too. Somewhere, his wife was calling or being called. She knew where he was. I didn't. I spent an agonizing hour before the phone rang. He'd been on a plane to Munich. I asked if he had called her first. He said no. I didn't believe him.

We met at a hotel a few days later. I cried and explained how I'd felt in that hour. *"Je ne le supporte pas,"* I said — I can't stand it. Not only that hour, all of it: lying next to my husband at night, listening to him breathe, the waiting for phone calls, the secret email accounts and deleted texts, the fabricating of last-minute meetings and dinners with friends, the rotten deception. He touched my cheek. He said he felt more lost than ever. Escaping death had made him want to be with me more, but it had also made him want to avoid being cruel to his wife.

"Tout a l'air si fragile maintenant," he said. Everything seems so fragile.

In the weeks after the attack, he was afraid, couldn't draw, sketched instead, didn't like that, tried to paint. "I've lost my

51

sense of irony," he said. "What's a political cartoonist without that?" I told myself that I wouldn't go back to him, and then I did. The hotels we stayed in afternoons were filled with tourists with cameras and guide-books and matching luggage. He and I had no bags. It was the same thing that we'd been doing for months; now it felt sordid. Now I cried with him as I cried with my husband, my head turned to the wall. Still, under the misery, was that feeling of being alive. This pain and guilt, this cork in my throat, this self-condemnation, seemed bet-ter than the fog of boredom, the certainty of what was around the bend.

Then, as happens in these stories, his wife found out in a cavalcade of clichés: my Metro card in his pocket, a credit card charge for a hotel, and of course not only that, but everything she knew about the change in the tide of their intimacy. He called me one night from a telephone booth. My husband was giving the children their bath. From down the hall came splashing and laughing.

"Elle sait tout," he said. She knows every-thing.

I said, *"Comment?"*

"I had to tell her. She'd figured it out."

"C'était qui?" my husband asked after I'd

52

hung up, and I — who had become so good at lying — said, *"Un faux numéro."*

I heard nothing for weeks. I felt grief like I hadn't known since my father died, an endless hole under my feet. There's a church down the street from the apartment my husband and I owned, with the thumb of Saint Anthony in a gold box. I only know Saint Anthony from the plaque under his relic, and I am not Catholic. During those weeks, though, I stopped in the chapel on my way home from work, kneeled in a pew, my head on my arms, and sobbed. I wish I could say that I was crying from guilt, but no, I was crying for him.

He called me again a month later, to say that he was sorry. He had perspective now. He loved his wife and always would. She was a *femme superbe,* and she had forgiven him. He hoped that I could come to love my husband again. If, he added, before hanging up, his wife ever came across me, could I do him one favor? He'd told her that he'd started to see me after the attack. He had framed our affair around that crisis. He'd confessed without confessing.

"Of course," I said. "If that's what you want."

I, on the other hand, that same night, told my husband everything. On the edge of our bed, I answered all of his questions. I felt an exquisite relief at the sight of his tears, at the way he raged, at the sound of the names he called me: *"salope," "menteuse."* I'd felt freed from my marriage since leaving the Metro with that number in my pocket. This freedom was sweeter, to be freed from my lies. "You're right," I told my husband. "I have no excuses." I agreed that we should separate. I knew what I'd ruined and that there was no going back. I thought, too, now that the initial shock and grief, the sobbing in the chapel, had ended, I would make another life, a third one. My children would come to my new apartment, which would be decorated in my style — whatever I found that to be — in a building with a view of a square. I'd make them American pancakes and *lardons* cut thick like bacon. I'd paint their rooms the colors they wanted, and we'd go to museums on Saturdays. I'd be that mother on the beach in Saint-Tropez with the two children and the picnic basket.

When we told them that we were divorcing, the children looked up from the couch with an incomprehension I've never seen on anyone's face. You mean *Maman* will not sleep here every night? Will we go to the mountains together still during the sum-

54

mer? Will we decorate a Christmas tree? Who will read us our bedtime story? Who will make our breakfast? Who will walk us to school? And the worst question: "Why?" Because your mother decided to climb on her bike and ride away somewhere else, having felt she'd circled here for too long. In my defense, I thought I was taking them with me.

One night, not long ago, the children with my ex-husband for the week, I sat at my computer looking up former classmates from high school in Chicago, old boyfriends, my roommate at Berkeley, fellow Tumbleweeds, my former lover, his wife, and, as the lights went on over the Seine, Olga and Hugo. He is still at Syracuse, an old man on a webpage who teaches literature and French grammar and a special topics course on the poetry of the French colonies. About Olga, I found nothing.

I looked up Rado Koto, a member of the French avant-garde, according to Wikipedia, a surrealist poet, a bisexual, who hanged himself in a hotel room not long after the publication of his second book of poetry. One website blamed Koto's suicide on his heroin addiction, another on his HIV status, another on his financial difficulties. Or maybe he suffered from clinical depression?

Who knows? In the year since my husband and I told our children that we were divorcing, I've learned that I know only one thing: when your children ask why, you want to give them a good answer.

The last name I looked up that night was the one that mattered the most. There is a woman named Élodie Boyer who works at a French school in New York, in charge of marketing. I am going to choose to think that she is the Élodie I once knew, that she is happy and healthy and still likes to watch birds, just as I choose to believe that my marriage ended because something called love went away, not that my husband and I would still be together if one afternoon I had chosen a different seat on the Metro. There's no going back from where I am now to say to Olga, I understand. "Silly girl," she said. "What can you possibly know about love?" I thought she was talking about Hugo.

ECLIPSE

1890

On the first of April, in the courtyard of the
Léger estate, Yvette Mongrain was scrubbing down the glass tables and wrought-
iron chairs that had been brought by train
from Paris the morning before and arranged
on the flagstones. A spring wind was on the
rise, whining through the bushes of the topiary and making the trees of the forest dance.
Tonight, by the time the foie gras and
oysters had been served and the wild boar
rolled out from the manor on its bed of
braised endive, the women's décolletages
would have erupted in goose bumps and
their husbands' noses gone pink. But none
of them, Yvette thought as she plunged her
rag into a bucket of water, would ask for
the wraps and overcoats hanging in the
manor. The rich never admitted to growing
hungry or lonely or cold.

   In the hard light of morning, the glass of

the table showed both of her chins, the squared lump of her nose and the wispy hair pinned tight to her head. She'd once been a slight girl with clear skin and a quick smile who seduced a procession of men before giving her heart to Gustave, the head gardener at the Léger estate. She'd been that girl when Monsieur Léger's father returned to his native village, after years spent overseeing the work of silkworms in China, accompanied by engineers and architects who chopped a road into the forest and cleared a space in the trees for the manor and a servants' cottage. She'd been that girl the day that she stood at the front door of the manor and lifted the brass lion head knocker, her references in the pocket of her well-mended coat, Gustave's good-luck kisses still warm on her neck. She was less of that girl when she walked with Gustave down the aisle of the church of Benneville and became even less with the birth of her son, who died after only a week, leaving her with swollen breasts and glossy trails down the sides of her waist. That was the same summer that the elder Monsieur Léger and his wife arrived at the manor with the colicky child whom Yvette had rocked through her own grief, whose first steps she'd applauded, whose picture books she had pretended to read, whose fevers she'd cooled, whose nose she'd wiped, whose tears she dried the summer that his mother left the house early, and the next summer when she didn't come at all. And now that child, this very morning, had looked down his no longer adorably stubby, now straight nose and told her that he'd seen out the window that the tables looked dirty and could she do something about it? The tables that she and the housemaid had spent hours scrubbing the previous afternoon.

"Glorious day, *n'est-ce pas?*"

Yvette looked up the façade of the manor. Three stories in the air, Madame Léger had come to her balcony in a fluttery dressing gown. Yvette didn't know if she was supposed to answer this question. Madame was always asking questions that seemed to require no answer. Are you glad, Yvette, that you never had children? Do you think my hands look older than they did last month? Do you ever feel, Yvette, as if you were drowning in an ocean and you can't remember how to swim? The night after Gustave died, having quivered with fever in bed for a week, Madame Léger knocked on the door of Yvette's room, holding a bouquet of jonquils.

"How dreadfully lonely you must feel,"

she said.

Her eyelashes beat back tears. Yvette stared at her dumbly, her hand on the doorknob, her bare feet cold on the floor. As the spicy scent of the jonquils floated past her into the shuttered room, where the smell of male sweat was already fading, she wanted to say that she and Gustave hadn't touched each other in more than ten years, hadn't even had the passion to fight, had built between themselves a wall of silence and that it was that wall that she missed, the sturdiness of it, not the airy things that she knew Madame Léger was imagining. Instead she said, *"Merci,"* and, after shutting and locking the door, shoved the bouquet under her mattress.

"I asked the housemaid to press your new gloves," she called up to the balcony. "I think you will need a stole. No doubt, it will be chilly tonight."

She was pleased that she'd said this, even though Madame Léger was no longer listening. She stared out at the forest, holding the railing, the black spindles patterning the white of her dressing gown. Yvette started on another table. The sun had changed position. In the glare of the glass she saw a faint suggestion of herself next to Madame

Léger's smeared reflection, which rose higher.

Yvette turned in time to see Madame Léger cascade into the air, down the creamy run of the façade, past the open windows of the second floor, the dressing gown billowing around her bare ankles like a failed parachute.

On the west side of the manor, in the rose garden, Pierre Frontin heard a wet thud and thought that a flower box had fallen from a window. Another mess he would have to clean up. He pinched a bruised petal from a Queen Elizabeth rose and dropped it on the ground. He was a thin young man with the articulations of a praying mantis and the tight face of a cockroach. His wife had sun-cured skin, breasts that were simply another roll of fat on her chest, and buttocks as white and lumpy as goat cheese. She wore men's boots under thick skirts, trimmed her nails with her teeth, and smelled of lye and regurgitated breast milk. So Pierre didn't have to worry about her sleeping with the postman when he was out. While Monsieur Léger was constantly having the trim of the manor repainted to mask the damage wreaked by storms and sun, the paint of the servants' cottage, where Pierre lived with his family, couldn't peel because there was no paint. The grass outside didn't need to be mowed because it was wild grass, meant to grow wild. He didn't have colleagues with high expectations. He didn't have a weak stomach from the stress of being important. He wasn't resented by the men who worked for him because no one worked for him. He wasn't stupid enough to host a *dîner en plein air* on the first day of April.

By now the tightness was gone from Pierre's throat. He even felt lucky as he moved around the bed of roses, noting the holes made in the leaves of the Louis Philippes by a still-nursing slug. When the elder Monsieur Léger was alive, bugs and rodents stayed out of the rose garden, and off the grounds of the estate. Even as an old man, his back so bent that his mustache nearly grazed the grass, Monsieur Léger, *père,* had walked spring and fall mornings through the gardens to the forest with his mushrooming basket. On his return, basket full, he'd stop to sit by the fountain, surrounded by the marble muses with their exposed breasts and frozen smiles, their offerings of lyres and harps and masks. *"C'est un paradis,"* he would say to Pierre as he looked out on the grounds. "I have been far and wide in this world. No place compares."

But his son, Monsieur Léger, *fils,* had no respect for the forest and so the forest had no respect for him. The summer that he arrived with his wife in their enormous carriage, the deer jumped the wall and devoured the lilies. Hawks and swallows pelted the flagstones of the courtyard, pine needles clogged the fountain, oak leaves littered the paths between the topiary bushes. The lives of the servants were consumed with erasing the forest's trash from the part of the estate that Monsieur Léger could see from the courtyard or from the back windows of the manor. Unlike his father, Monsieur Léger never walked the grounds, and you could for this reason get away with things. You could, for instance, prune only the side of the bushes that faced the house. Monsieur Léger wanted things to look nice, not necessarily to be nice.

Pierre flicked the slug off the leaf and moved on to the Bourbon roses. When he'd worked for the elder Monsieur Léger, he would have crushed the slug between his fingers, searched the rest of the plant, and drawn a ring of salt around the roots. He would have never thought to cut corners. Every morning, shears in hand, he walked the path of the topiary, checking the curve of a vase, the roofline of the pagoda, the complicated upward sweep of the dog's tail, the dip that made the shape in its mouth resemble a bone. He knew that the elder Monsieur Léger, from the windows of his study, could see Pierre working so hard and with such precision. He believed, as he had once believed his mother's stories about forest gnomes and fairies, that this recurring sight would result in his being mentioned in Monsieur Léger's will, that he could pick and pluck and prune his way into a life like the one Monsieur Léger, *fils,* led at his fancy Parisian school. All day long he worked beside Gustave, whose rants and wheezy sighs filled him with pity. Think, he wanted to say, of the tulips that rise from the iron-poor soil in the beds at the side of the manor, the rhododendron that rerooted itself after being torn from the ground by a boar, the chestnut tree that grows on, into the sky, despite the fungus that must be scraped from its bark every spring. He'd tried once to explain these thoughts to Gustave as they sat together in the rose garden, sharing a sausage and a round of Brie. In response, the old man lowered his hat over his eyes, let out a belch, and rolled onto his back for his afternoon nap.

Then, one evening, the elder Monsieur

Léger collapsed, face-first, into his plate of *quenelles,* leaving everything to his son, who hadn't been to visit the estate in years. All through that fall, winter, and spring, Pierre continued to manicure the grounds with the same rigorous tenderness. When Monsieur Léger rode up to the manor the next summer in his carriage, he wore a sharp mustache over a tight mouth, and his wife wore furs even though it was June. Monsieur Léger called Pierre into his father's study. With a sour glance at Pierre's boots, he said that the peony beds at the front of the manor were as fussy as death and should be ripped out, and that he wanted the topiary cut into modern, geometrical forms.

"We must drag this pile of rocks out of the last century," he said. "I don't want my guests thinking I'm a stuffed shirt."

That afternoon, as Pierre dug up the peonies, minding not to damage the roots so he could replant them in front of his cottage, Gustave walked by with a bucket of concrete for a crack in the fountain.

"Stop caring so much," Gustave said with a grunt. "It will get you nowhere."

Pierre wasn't a stupid man. He recognized that Gustave had cared so little that he had walked home from the café in Benneville in a rainstorm, and caught a cold from which

65

he never recovered. You needed, he had decided, only to care enough to survive.

He collected the roses and dumped them behind the potting shed. As he walked around the side of the manor toward the courtyard, past the triangles and squares of the topiary, he wondered whether the unfortunate flowerpot was the clay one with hideous faces carved on the front that Monsieur Léger had brought back from some country in Africa. Rounding the corner, he saw Yvette looking down at a white mass, one hand on her hip, a rag dripping from the other.

On the east side of the manor, Dominique, the chore boy, sat in the chestnut tree, his legs dangling down either side of a branch. So far he'd heard and seen nothing, save a loud thump and a squirrel with a crooked tail. He was beginning to think that he'd chosen the wrong tree. Madame Léger had said the big tree with the twisted branches, but he wondered if she'd meant the oak tree that stood behind the topiary.

She'd come to him the day before as he worked in the potting shed, cutting a pine plank in two. She wore a liquid dress with a low-cut bodice. When she said his name from the doorway, the saw grazed the flesh

66

above his knee.

"Viens, s'il te plaît." She turned back toward the manor. "I need you. A plant is dying."

Dominique hurried behind Madame Léger, his leg stinging, the saw shrilling in his hand until, not knowing where else to put it, he dropped it on the grass. He followed her through the servants' entrance to the manor, along the tiles to the oak floors, where the walls changed from paint to shimmering silk, up the marble staircase, down a hall covered with paintings of Monsieur Léger: Monsieur Léger, a wide-eyed baby on his mother's lap, Monsieur Léger, a toddler in front of his father's factory, a young man flanked by whippets, astride an elephant, kissing the hand of the pope, in the basket of a *montgolfière,* to a foyer, where Madame Léger stopped next to a set of long windows and pointed at a fern with tobacco-colored fronds.

"I tell the housemaid to give it water," she said. "Who knows if she does. *La pauvre plante a l'air de plus en plus misérable.*"

"It needs more light." Dominique dragged the ceramic pot closer to the windows. Madame Léger watched him with a distracted smile, her shoulder blades balanced on the wall, the rest of her body dripping

67

toward the floor. As he snapped a skeletal frond from the fern, Dominique glimpsed for the first time a misshapen tooth at the corner of Madame Léger's smile, gray and melted-looking, before her lips shut down and she brushed by him toward a nearby door.

"You should take a look at my husband's cactus," she said.

In Monsieur Léger's study, a globe sat on a pedestal next to a desk with brass hinges, the only spots of light in the room, since the curtains were closed. On the windowsill, a cactus bolted from a pot. While Dominique prodded the soil, Madame Léger opened the liquor cabinet and took out a bottle of cognac. She set two glasses on Monsieur Léger's desk, then filled each one to just under the rim.

"Did you know?" she said, after taking a sip, "that there was a drink named after me once? 'Gisèle's tears,' it was called. Funny, since I never used to cry."

Dominique shook his head, although he did indeed know about the drink. He had heard all of the stories at the servants' table regarding Madame Léger's past as a courtesan, a "slut dressed like a lady," Yvette liked to say. She'd ride afternoons through the Parc des Buttes-Chaumont in a lemon-colored carriage, her hair dyed to match. In her apartment over the Seine, she had a caged parakeet that sang dirty songs and a secret cupboard to hide her lovers when their wives came knocking. She'd been served naked, sprinkled with parsley, to a cousin of the emperor. Now, though, her décolleté was cracked like the varnish of her husband's desk, and her chin wanted to meet her neck.

Dominique wiped the soil from his fingers on the sleeve of his shirt. He gulped the cognac, watching the open door.

"Don't fret," Madame Léger said. "He is out shooting. He spends the first four hours trying to locate the trigger." She licked the rim of her glass and set it back on the desk. "He ordered a boar from the Vosges for tomorrow night's dinner. He may be a poor huntsman but he is not stupid."

Dominique tried not to smile. He'd once assisted Monsieur Léger on a hunt with a guest. Monsieur Léger marched over the pine needles and oak leaves, describing in a too-loud voice how he'd hunted big game in Africa and crocodiles on the Amazon. When a fox darted from its den, Monsieur Léger shot a log. Another time, Monsieur Léger had asked Dominique to come along on a mushrooming expedition meant to impress a man from the national senate who was from the coast and thus knew nothing about mushrooms. Monsieur Léger couldn't tell a chanterelle from a morel. By the end of the outing, he'd tossed several poisonous mushrooms into the senator's basket. That evening the senator was driven away by fast carriage, sour-faced and retching as, in the kitchen, Monsieur Léger berated the cook for having undercooked the *porc à la moutarde* and "giving a great man worms."

Madame Léger sat down on a leather couch. "Tell me something," she said.

Dominique set his glass on the desk. "Nothing has ever happened to me. So I don't have much to tell."

"I felt that way when I was your age," Madame Léger said. "I was very poor, you know. To be poor in Paris is not pleasant. *Mais j'étais déterminée.*" She patted the couch. "I've seen you watch me at my husband's parties. I've looked out the window and found your face in the bushes."

Dominique thought of the swirl of Madame Léger's hips as she danced by the window, her cheek crushed against a lapel, her bored mouth. He sat down next to her and put his hand on her knee. She knocked it off.

"Ne sois pas ridicule," she said.

She got up and walked to the door. On the threshold, as Dominique hurried away, she caught his arm and whispered that he should sit in the branches of the big tree behind the house the next morning, at ten fifteen precisely.

Madame Léger's eyes were open and unblinking. Her nose trembled with the breath that entered her body in a shudder and left in a sigh.

"I think she's trying to say something," Pierre said.

"Elle ne dit rien," Yvette said. "She's in that moment between life and death when there's nothing to say."

The rag in her hand had soaked her left knee through her dress. She couldn't let it go. She stared at Madame Léger's forehead and remembered how Gustave would turn his back to her as he undressed in the evening, the wiry hairs on his shoulders, the puckered skin of his waist. She hadn't cried in so long that her tears were crusty with salt. Pierre reached over to take her hand. On the stones below, the blood from Madame Léger's head was forking into a crimson tree.

As she stared past Pierre and Yvette at the liquid sky, Madame Léger had never felt so

71

peaceful. The pain had lifted away, and now she floated in a bath that would never grow cold. She thought about the chore boy watching from the tree. One night, years from now, his wife would wake up to the sound of sobs. After she shook him out of his dream, he'd tell her about the beautiful woman whom he had once loved.

"Look," Yvette said.

A shadow was spreading from the roof of the manor, blotting out the sky as it went.

When the sun disappeared, Monsieur Léger was at his desk, adding to his list. He got up from the chair and peeled back a curtain. He could barely make out the long run of the drive and the shaggy roof of the forest. He'd seen this happen once before, during his childhood. He was walking the wall between the manor and the trees when the world went black. He tried to climb down, but he couldn't find a foothold and tumbled over the edge. His heart in a fist, he followed the line of trunks, twisting his ankle and falling twice into brambles until he came to the gate. As he stumbled over the lawn, his mother ran out of the manor. She crushed his head to her stomach and listed all of the horrible things that she thought had happened to him.

"Plus jamais," she said. "Never vanish again."

This was not long before she herself started to vanish. She would wander the rose garden without her hat, sit in the pergola for hours, never turning a page in her book, kiss him on the forehead rather than the cheek, until one morning she left for Switzerland to take the waters and didn't come back.

Monsieur Léger inched through the darkness to the door of his study and out into the hall.

"Hello," he called. "Where is everyone?"

On the stairs, he took the treads one by one. When his slippers slapped on the landing, he reached out for the wall and moved his hand across the cool surface until his fingers stubbed on the door trim of the dining room. Next to the lines of the butler's pantry a light glowed from the kitchen. He pushed open the door. The cook sprawled in front of the stove, smoking a cigarette. Above his head, tendrils of gas licked the bottoms of shadowy pots. Monsieur Léger shuffled closer. The cook looked up, his face a circle marked by three splotches.

"A fine pickle." He blew out a curl of smoke.

"C'est une éclipse," Monsieur Léger said.

"Nothing to worry about. I'm looking for my wife. Have you seen her?"

"I can't say that I have. I can't say that I haven't. It is quite dark, *vous savez, monsieur.*"

"I can smell your caramel burning," Monsieur Léger said. He turned and made his way back into the hall. He tried to conjure up what exactly the cook looked like, whether his eyes were as beady as he remembered and his eyebrows as high. He would fire the man tomorrow. Gisèle wouldn't be happy about it, but the season was almost over. She could make onion soup and omelets like the ones she used to make him in her apartment on the Left Bank. "You are the only one for me now," she would say as she fed him a bite.

He found the handle of the front door. Outside, the sky was cloudless, the birds silent, the forest a tangle of shadows. He walked down the steps, holding the metal railing. His right foot crunched on the gravel of the drive. Along the side of the manor, he called his wife's name. Once he found her, he'd bring her into his study to show her his list: the scarf on the floor of the third-floor guestroom last month, the foggy stain of her naked shoulders against the French doors, the paper she'd used to slip a note into the pocket of a visiting duke at last week's tea, the bisecting rings on the edge of his desk yesterday afternoon. Tonight, he would tell her, would not be so easy. Tonight there would be no trips to powder her nose just as the viscount of such and such went down the hall for his coat, no twenty-minute expeditions to the kitchen to ask for a raspberry to drop into her *coupe de champagne.* This time she'd be surrounded by the emptiness between the courtyard and the house, and she wouldn't pass through it without him at her side.

From above, a shape slid out of a tree.

"I'm looking for my wife," Monsieur Léger said. "Have you seen her?"

"An enormous bird rose from the forest and ate the sun."

Monsieur Léger couldn't see the boy's face, but he could smell his fear.

"Imbécile," he said. "The sun always returns."

He called out again for his wife, louder this time, and continued through the courtyard, past the topiary, toward the rose garden. Something sharp grazed his heel. He cursed but didn't stop. Behind the pergola, a wall of bushes grew at his side, barbed and shapeless, as if they had never been trimmed.

A PLACE IN THE COUNTRY

1980

It was their weekend in the country, which meant a weekend with Jacques's parents in their cottage outside of Benneville. This was not exactly the country — Benneville had grown since Jacques was a boy, moving closer to Paris on a wave of concrete, and it would not be a true weekend but rather one day, split in two, and one night. At his job in Paris, Jacques did a lot of counting, "living life by spreadsheet," as his wife, Hélène, liked to put it, and already, an hour into the visit, he had started the countdown to tomorrow morning at eleven, when the car would be packed with their bags and with a box of the vegetables he was currently helping his father to harvest from his garden. Jacques's sons were in the garden as well: Alexis in the shallot bed and Emmanuel with the cabbages. Each boy had a basket, as Jacques did. He was in charge of the leeks, although the person truly in charge here was Jacques's father, Henri.

"Don't yank," Henri said. "Pull."

Six tufting rows of Batavia lettuce away, he was talking to Alexis, Jacques's smallest son, and not only small because he was six to Emmanuel's seven. Alexis had come out tiny, two point five kilos, and now, crouched as he was under Jacques's father, he resembled a gargoyle under a church steeple. At almost seventy, Henri had maintained his schoolmaster posture; his gardening cloak swept toward the ground from 180-degree shoulders. He leaned over to show Alexis the proper twist-pull method for harvesting vegetables and began to lecture about roots, pointing to those on the shallot he had pulled, explaining capillaries, the importance of removing all parts of the plant from the soil. *"Sans ses racines,"* he said, "a plant has nothing to connect it to the world."

"But why do we need to take out the roots if we're going to eat the shallots anyway?" Alexis asked innocently. Henri winced. Jacques and his brother, Guy, had grown up in the schoolmaster's house behind the Benneville *école de garçons,* and during their primary years, their father had also been their teacher. Jacques had seen Henri wince like that often when a boy asked a

seemingly obvious question, followed —
here it came — by a quick, raspy laugh.

"It is true," Henri told Alexis, "that we
are going to eat them anyway. Yet is that a
reason to do something *à moitié*?" He
pointed at the ground. "Look at the mess
you've left."

"I think what your grandfather means,"
Jacques called to Alexis, "is that it's not a
good idea to leave old roots in the dirt."

Guy had invented this technique: *la diversion.* When one of them got in trouble with
their father, the other one would create a
bigger problem. If Guy did poorly on a
school assignment, Jacques would make
sure to fail the next day's *test d'orthographe.*
If one of them asked to do something that
was against their father's principles — like
join the Boy Scouts — the other would ask
to do something worse, like become an altar
boy. Once, after Jacques broke a glass in the
kitchen, Guy threw a *pétanque* ball through
the front window.

"No," Henri said to Jacques. "That is not
what I mean."

"I could use a shovel," Alexis said.

"It's called a trowel," Jacques's father said.
"And one should not need to use one."

"*C'est l'heure du goûter,* anyway," Jacques
said. *La diversion* hadn't worked. It was time

for a *dispersion.*

"Didn't they just have lunch?" Henri said. *"Eh ben."* He sighed. "Yes, you boys go in. Your father and I will finish up here." He looked over at Emmanuel. "That one isn't getting anything done anyway." Emmanuel had wandered away from the cabbages and was pursuing a butterfly in the brussels sprouts, tightrope walking one of the wooden planks that lined the beds. Jacques called to him that it was time for a snack, and he whooped off toward the gate, yelling at Alexis to come.

"Go on with your brother," Jacques said to Alexis.

"I can finish this row first."

"Clearly, you cannot." Jacques's father took his basket. "You missed three shallots right over there."

Alexis watched his grandfather stride away with the basket. His chin trembled. When Henri had suggested that the boys come with them to the garden, Jacques had feared a moment like this one.

"Vite," he said. "Run away while he's gone."

Alexis pushed up his glasses. *"D'accord,"* he said mournfully. He slumped off toward the gate, where Emmanuel waited. He hadn't understood that Jacques was making a joke, and he wouldn't have understood the joke anyway. Alexis, like Jacques, didn't have much of a sense of humor. *Il n'a aucun sens de l'humour,* Jacques had heard Hélène say on the phone to one of her friends, years ago, and Jacques knew that she was talking about him. He found jokes difficult, and most conversation exhausting; this was one of the reasons that he and Hélène were good together, because she was adept at the art of small talk, of asking questions that got people talking instead of looking at you oddly, wondering what you'd meant. Her anger was deep, her laughter deep, and when she was sad, as she'd been the year her mother died, she sobbed all of a sudden, anywhere — the bank line, the market, the cinema. "So what if people know I'm crying," she would snap when Jacques gave her a tissue. "Better to be overly emotional than to have no emotions." When they were first dating, she had made Jacques talk about his feelings all the time, to the point that it felt like a persecution. "It isn't that I don't feel what you feel," he'd said. "It's only that I feel it more quietly."

Jacques finished the leeks while his father sprayed the endives with something called Rotenone — he was generous with pesticides and considered organic gardening a luxury of the *bourgeoisie*. Then they took the baskets along the perfectly graveled pathway, past the perfectly sculpted rows, stopped to drop the spent husks and withered leaves into the steaming compost pile ("Forty degrees," his father said. "It's the new worms."), went through the gate and over the perfectly mowed grass. When Jacques's father had retired to the cottage, Jacques wondered what he would do with his time, after all those years spent running the school in Benneville, being on the village council, coaching the boys' *équipe de foot*. The answer came that first spring, when his father's patch of watercress became a plot of watercress and lettuce, mâche, and strawberries. Over the years, the garden had essentially turned into a small farm, with crops rotated by season, tepees for the cucumbers and tomatoes, trellises for the green beans, raised beds, flat beds, rare species such as the *potiron turban* and *melon noir des Carmes,* and pieces of slate from a broken chalkboard marking the name of each plant.

At the back of the cottage, they took the baskets to the vegetable room, a onetime coal room that Jacques's father had converted into his workspace.

"How did those boys manage to trail dirt

on the landing?" his father asked.

He pointed at a crumbly trail that led over the tiles toward the hall and the rest of the house. Jacques didn't answer. Henri went through the world commenting on what didn't work, and Jacques had learned to ignore most of what he said. It was a technique he had developed with Guy, when his brother started to speak nonsensically.

They took off their boots, and Jacques put on his loafers — "city shoes," his father called them — as his father hung his gardening cloak on a hook. They washed their hands at the utility sink with the plug of soap impaled on a rod. Braids of shallots and onions dangled from the ceiling. On the walls were shelves of reclaimed jam jars filled with the pickles and preserves Jacques's mother made: cornichons, pearl onions, strawberry, blackberry, raspberry jam. In a corner, a deep freezer hummed. During the first years of the garden, Jacques and Hélène would return from their visits with boxes and boxes of beets, cabbages, heads of lettuce, turnips, and leeks, which Hélène called "vulgar onions."

"How can one man produce this many vegetables?" she had said as they tried to make room in their refrigerator. "I feel like Sisyphus."

Then, one Christmas, she had thought to buy his parents a deep freezer for the vegetable room. "Now nothing will go to waste," she told Jacques's father, who was delighted. It was Hélène's genius to be able to get what she wanted and make everyone else think that they were getting what they wanted, even that she was being self-sacrificing.

"Amène ces poireaux à ta mère," Jacques's father said, handing Jacques two leeks. "She needed some for tonight's dinner. I'll put together a box of vegetables for you and one for your brother."

"He won't want it," Jacques said.

"Your mother likes him to have it."

"All right, then," Jacques said. "If you say so."

Tomorrow, he would call Guy and say that he had a box of vegetables that he could drop by. Guy would say that he didn't like vegetables, and that Jacques was the one with a family to feed. Guy lived alone in a suburban apartment that looked out on a municipal dump. He worked in the kitchen of an Arche Cafétéria off the *autoroute*. He hadn't been to see his parents in ten years. He'd never visited the cottage. Jacques had last seen Guy with his parents on a Christmas before the boys were born. Guy stayed in the house behind the school with Hélène and Jacques's mother, smoking and watching TV, his arms hanging down the sides of the chair. He slurped up his oysters and ate his *foie gras* off his knife, took a walk to the Seine, kissed everyone goodbye, then got in his dinged-up car and drove away. These days, Jacques saw Guy twice a year, when he went to the Blimpy and bought him dinner. Over *pommes frites* and leathery *escalope de dinde,* he told Guy about the boys and his job. Guy would grunt occasionally, pour more water into his glass, dunk his *frite* in the gravy. He had sweat stains above his ears on the paper cap he left on his head and, when he was having one of his reactions to his medication, amoeba-shaped hives on his neck.

Jacques left his father in the vegetable room and took the leeks down the hall. The cottage had only two bedrooms, upstairs, cut into triangles by the eaves, with a bathroom in the middle. Downstairs was a large sitting room with a stone fireplace and a blip of a kitchen that looked out on the garden. Jacques's parents had painted the main room when they bought the cottage, but the soot and grease on the walls had bled through in splotches. After the pipes in the upstairs bathroom leaked, they'd installed a drop ceiling. There was a couch that converted for the boys to sleep on, a small TV, and, jammed against the window, the dining room table that had stood in the schoolmaster's house. The kitchen still had its original ceramic sink and a hodgepodge of pipes that led outside to the well and brought back water that tasted of metal and stone. Jacques found the cottage dark and dingy and cramped, but Hélène said that with a thick coat of paint and recessed lights, the drop ceilings torn away to show the original beams, the rotted window frames replaced and the fireplace bricked, it would be *charmante comme tout.* She had pulled up a corner of carpet in the guest-room and found, to her delight, rough-hewn pine floors, which, finished and polished, would look very "chic."

In the kitchen, Hélène and Jacques's mother were at the Formica table, peeling carrots and potatoes onto a sheet of newspaper. Although she wore no makeup, Hélène looked as if she did, her cheeks flushed and her eyes bright, the lashes long and singularly defined. Sometimes, even now, Jacques would walk into a room and stop to look at her, amazed that he had ended up with this person.

"Papa thought you'd want these for tonight," he said. He put the leeks on the table. Yes, his mother said, she and Hélène were going to make "a nice little *poêlée de poireaux*" to go with the *gigot,* trimmed perfectly for her by the butcher Marcel, and the *"bons petits champignons"* that Jacques's father would go find in the forest after his nap. She wrapped the carrot and potato peelings in the sheet of newspaper for the compost pile.

Hélène took the leeks to the sink. "You have some dirt on your cheek," she said to Jacques as she passed by. His mother reached up and brushed it off. Her thin hair was permed into tight curls, her face chalky with the pancake makeup she used to hide the broken capillaries on her nose, which was as long and thin as a shark fin. Jacques, like her, had a large nose, his rounder and thicker, a square jaw like his father, and hair that tended to bushiness. Although he and Guy were fraternal twins, they looked nothing alike. Guy had apparently inherited the recessive genes in the family: his hair was red and his skin pale and freckled — he burned easily, and when he was upset, his face flamed. Even before his illness fully showed, he had been quick to anger, unlike Jacques, and considered "off" and "strange" by the other boys. There had been a persistent rumor at school that he wasn't really Jacques's twin and had been secretly adopted.

"How are Alexis and Emmanuel?" Jacques asked Hélène.

"They seem fine." Hélène was washing the leeks, gold bracelets clinking. "They're upstairs in our room. Your mother found a game for them."

"Your old peg solitaire," Jacques's mother said. "Remember how you and Guy used to love to play?"

The rest of the afternoon went by pleasantly enough. The boys were, indeed, playing peg solitaire in the upstairs bedroom, and Alexis seemed perfectly fine. Jacques did a sudoku as his mother did a crossword. Hélène embroidered. When Henri came back with the mushrooms, there was the usual scurry, then they all settled back into their seats. At six, night fell, and they had their kirs and aperitif biscuits by the fireplace, as the boys drank the Oranginas that Jacques's mother kept for their visits. Henri made a fire, burned the newspaper, the paper in which the butcher had wrapped the *gigot*, and the silver wrapping from the box of chocolates that Hélène had brought from Paris. Jacques's mother set a pan of chestnuts in the flames for the boys. Henri poured himself a second kir. He said several things that were incorrect about inflation and Valéry Giscard d'Estaing's policies and the strikes taking place that month. Jacques listened and nodded and had a second kir too. He counted his father's inaccuracies. When Henri started in on the national deficit, Hélène raised her eyebrows at Jacques, an expression that said: We are in this together. Jacques possessed a degree in math and another in economics. He was a *fonctionnaire de catégorie A* at the Ministère de l'Economie et des Finances. And here was his father lecturing him about the deficit as if Jacques were a hairdresser or a professor of the visual arts. But what can you do with someone like that? Hélène would say — one of her favorite expressions.

"The most recent numbers are lower than that, actually," Jacques said, and his father shook his head.

"Even if they are" — and then he was on to the benefits of Marxism, where he always ended up.

Still, as the fire burned and the chestnuts let off their steamy, meaty smell, and the kirs softened the edges, Jacques felt affection for his father, this stern *homme de principes* from a retreating world. The same tenacity that Henri Havre displayed in his vegetable garden had made him a local hero during the war, which he'd spent passing messages in his schoolmaster's bag. When the Americans bombed Benneville, he was lying with both legs broken in a Gestapo cell. And Jacques felt terribly in love with Hélène as the shadows of the fire flowed over her face, and in love with his boys, on their stomachs in front of the television, watching an American Western. He took another handful of aperitif biscuits from the box his mother passed him. There were only fifteen hours left of this visit, and he would be asleep for eight of them.

But then, as they sat at the table with the *gigot* and pans of sautéed leeks, caramelized tomatoes from the freezer, and mushrooms from the forest, Jacques's father started in again on the boys. Hélène had admired the flavor of the leeks, and said that Jacques's father had such the green hand, and Jacques's father said, "It was not passed down to your children," with one of his ironic smiles that felt like the cut of a switchblade. He pointed his fork at Emmanuel.

"That one barely got a cabbage out of the ground before he was off to chase butterflies." He pivoted the fork. "And this one thought the parsley was lettuce."

He went on to describe the shallots with the broken roots, and the "yanking as if pulling a tooth." Emmanuel didn't seem to have heard his grandfather's insults — everything rolled off of him. But Alexis's chin trembled.

Hélène patted his shoulder and simultaneously grabbed Emmanuel's hand to stop him from mining out the inside of his piece of baguette and rolling it into a ball. She was sitting between them. Jacques was on the other side of the table, his parents at each head.

"They live in Paris," Jacques said to his father.

"Have some more of the nice little tomatoes from the garden," Jacques's mother said. She leaned across the table to scoop another spoonful onto Alexis's plate.

"Wherever they live, they are old enough to know the difference between parsley and lettuce," Henri said.

"I like eating bread this way," Emmanuel whispered to Hélène.

"You are making a mess all over the table," she whispered back.

"It's all right," Jacques's mother said. "We will shake the cloth off outside for the birds. Would you help me, Alexis?"

"The next time we visit," Jacques said to

Henri, "we won't have the boys help in the garden."

"So that's what you're teaching them? To give up?" Henri passed the green salad to Alexis. "Eat some," he said. "Your grandmother put your shallots in the dressing. You will improve. You and I will go out together alone next time."

All through the next course, into dessert, Jacques ate quietly as Hélène cast warning glances across the table. Alexis's chin stilled again. Jacques's mother sent him and Emmanuel to the freezer for homemade strawberry sorbet that they ate with ladyfingers. Jacques's throat felt frozen even before he took a spoonful. This was not the same room he'd sat in for dinner as a boy, although the puce paint color was the same, and so was the wax tablecloth. Still, it seemed that Alexis was he and Emmanuel was Guy. Or the opposite. It wasn't clear. What *was* clear was that his father was a bully. A hero, maybe, but also a bully. Nothing was ever or would ever be enough for him. He used to stand behind Guy's chair, making him sit still as he did his homework. "Stop moving your leg," he would say. "Focus." When Guy doodled on his *cahier* — sketches of jellyfish rising over a forest, a man with two heads, a skeleton holding an umbrella, their father ripped out the pages. At fifteen, when Guy began to string random words together — *apple, lamb, bicycle, moon* — their father said, "Stop, and make a sentence. No, that is not a proper sentence. *Sujet. Verbe.*" The next year, when Guy started to hear voices, their father said that he'd indulged his imagination too much and removed all of the books from the house. When Guy cut his palms with a razor, their father started to shave in the schoolhouse and locked the kitchen knives in the trunk of his car. Jacques knew that it didn't make sense to think that Guy wouldn't have gone crazy if their father had let him go crazy, but sitting at the table, watching Alexis eat his sorbet, he remembered that hopeless feeling of watching his brother become someone his father couldn't stand.

"What is wrong with you?" Hélène whispered that night as they sat in bed under the slick run of a sateen comforter. "You aren't acting like yourself at all. You're picking fights with your father."

"Did you see how he's treating Alexis?"

"He's being who he always is. Alexis is reacting to you. We all are. *Tu es stressé, donc il est stressé.*"

She was twisting her hair into the knot

she wore to sleep, her head tilted against the slant of the ceiling. He could see the outline of her breast through her nightgown. He moved down in the bed and touched the small of her back. She shook her head.

"Your parents will hear. They're right next door and your father is awake half the night going to the bathroom."

They wouldn't hear anything, though, because Hélène no longer made a sound when they had sex. Jacques watched her squeeze a meringue of lotion into the palm of her hand, braiding it between her fingers.

"Let's go home early tomorrow," he said. "I can't do another eleven hours."

She slid down next to him in the bed, smelling of violets. "I know it's hard. Your father, *c'est un homme impossible.*" She moved her hips against his. "You need to stay patient," she said. "Here's what wouldn't make sense: We put up with your father for all these years, and then you antagonize him and he changes his will and we don't get the cottage." Hélène reached into his boxers and rubbed her thumb along the ridge of his penis, working his erection.

"He wouldn't do that. And I don't know why you want this house so much, anyway."

"Because it's the only way we will ever afford a place in the country."

She kissed him to stop him from talking. She was managing him, he knew, but he succumbed. As she stroked him, he thought of how it would be, their place in the country with the rooms painted white and the heavy furniture gone and his father's vegetable garden replaced by a patio. Their friends from Paris would visit, drink kirs, count the stars, wander off to the forest with walking sticks and cardigans slung over their shoulders. Maybe he could convince Guy to come for a weekend and sleep in this guest-room under the skylight that Hélène planned to punch into the roof.

"Papa is going to die at one hundred, you know," he said.

"I don't think so. Not with his high blood pressure. Your mother told me the doctor is concerned."

"That's a terrible thing to say." He stopped her hand.

"I didn't mean it that way," she said. "And I'm only expressing what we're both think-ing."

"No, you aren't." He turned to his side. *"Bonne nuit."*

The next morning, he slept late. When he came down the hall, his mother was ironing napkins at the dining room table. She told him that Hélène had gone to mass. "The boys were up early. They're outside, and Henri's in the garden."

She got him a bowl of coffee and *biscottes* with raspberry preserves. She asked him about work, his recent promotion.

"Have you seen your brother lately?" She poured more coffee into his bowl.

"About a month ago. He has a dog now."

His mother smiled. "It's good that he has a dog."

Jacques knew that she meant it was good because it suggested that Guy could have a dog with no harm coming to the dog. Their mother had been the one to find the skinned cat in Guy's armoire. Jacques was in his first year at university, Guy having dropped out of school, and his mother called him at the dormitory. "Your father has had your brother taken away in an ambulance, and he won't tell me where."

Now Jacques's mother patted his arm. "You'll bring him his vegetables and he'll know I'm thinking of him," she said.

Hélène came into the kitchen, unwinding a scarf from her neck. "You're up, finally," she said. "I should start packing. Emmanuel has fencing lessons this afternoon. Where are the boys?"

"Outside," Jacques's mother said.

"I didn't see them." She pulled off her

gloves, one finger at a time.

"I'll go," Jacques said. He was glad that last night's fight seemed to be over. He looked for Alexis and Emmanuel in front of the cottage and down the road, and then went around back to the garden, where his father was cutting dead raspberry brambles from the fence.

"I told them to take a walk in the forest," he said when Jacques asked if he'd seen the boys. "They were running around the lawn like lunatics."

"You sent them to the forest alone?"

"I didn't send them. I suggested they go."

"How long have they been out there?"

"I don't know. *Une heure?*"

"They're probably lost."

"I told them exactly where to go. I said stay on the logging road. Don't take the trail to the pond. You and your brother used to go there all the time. You're being overly protective."

Jacques looked back at his father, throat frozen again. This was what always happened. Even now. Even when Jacques was almost forty years old, had people constantly knocking on his office door to ask him how to do this or do that, balance that spreadsheet, explain that figure. Every time he thought that he was right, his father said something that made that feeling turn to sand. "I needed to make a decision," he had said about Guy. "He killed a cat. He was hurting himself. He could have hurt someone else. And if I'd asked you or your mother first, you would have said no."

Jacques had taken the train to Benneville from his university, and the three of them drove up the road to the mental hospital, which was housed in a former convent. Hands on the wheel, Jacques's father laid out the procedure done to Guy the day before, how it would help, the statistics, what the doctors had told him. "It is much like resetting a clock," he said, "so that it ticks the right time." Jacques had tried to explain it to Emmanuel and Alexis once. As he started, he stopped, because it was too terrible. A doctor pushed a spike into your uncle's eye socket. He detached one part of his brain from another. The idea was to make him stop getting upset, yelling over nothing, hearing voices that told him to do strange things like take off his clothes and stand in the square, or trap stray cats and skin them. He was awful to be with, your uncle. That's the truth. He frightened me. I was glad to be away from him at school. I wished that those schoolyard rumors had been true and he wasn't really my twin, that

97

he'd been adopted into the family, that I didn't share his blood.

But the surgery didn't work as it was supposed to, or maybe it worked too well. I walked into the hospital room with my parents, and the boy in the bed looking at me with those flat eyes wasn't my brother. My brother was full of ideas, and before they became crazy, they had often been wonderful. When we were little, we would go to the forest after school. We started to run as we passed the old mill, Guy always ahead, slapping the tree trunks, counting them off. We chased rabbits and foxes. We climbed the trees and tried to see Paris. We swam in the pond and dived toward the bottom, looking for the rifle supposedly lost there by two brothers out hunting at the start of the century. We came back up together, took a breath, then pummeled our way back through the water again. "It has to be there," Guy would say after I'd given up and swum to the bank. And then down he'd go again, kicking and splashing. I see now that this was the beginning of him hearing and seeing things that didn't exist, but at the time I envied his determination.

"Hélène wants to get on the road," Jacques said. He turned away from the fence. "I'll go find the boys."

"I'll come with you," his father said, "so you don't get lost looking."

Jacques waited for his father to put the clippers back in the shed, and they walked up the drive past the manor. "Olga's having the roof patched," Henri said of the men hammering the slate. "She does what she can when she can." Jacques thought, as he had before, that his father had moved to this property because here he could remember every day that he had been on the right side during the war.

"*Et voilà,*" his father said when they'd entered the forest and turned onto the logging road. "Right there as I told you they'd be."

The boys weren't alone. They were standing with the driver of a truck that tilted off the road with the left tire in a drainage ditch. Jacques knew the man right away from his shoulder, which slumped so much that his hand hung almost to his knee. Quasimodo, the kids used to call him. Tin Back, Soldier Boy.

"What has Louis done now?" his father said.

Jacques called to the boys and they came running.

"We were over there" — Alexis pointed toward a trail near a pyramid of logs — "and we heard a noise."

"His tires slipped," Emmanuel said.

"We told him we could help him push it out."

"Maybe we could use a rope or something?"

"How did you manage that?" Jacques's father said to Louis Nevers, who was looking into the ditch, at the current of water running between the tires.

"Je ne sais pas," he said glumly.

Jacques said hello. Louis and Guy had been friends, before Guy stopped having friends, sharing the bond of social outcasts. They'd fallen out, Jacques remembered, when Guy and Jacques were ten, after Guy convinced Louis that they should lay centimes — or was it francs? — on the train tracks that ran behind the village church. One afternoon, Guy stormed into the kitchen, where Jacques was doing his homework. He paced in front of the refrigerator, furious. He told Jacques how he and Louis had put the coins on the tracks, and how, after the train had gone by, they were nowhere to be found. "Louis took them," Guy said. "I know he did. He's a cripple witch thief." *Handicapé sorcier voleur.* He raged and raged. Jacques said he doubted Louis stole the coins. They had probably flown far from the weight of the train. He went with Guy to the tracks to calm him down. They couldn't see any coins in the gravel. Guy kicked the rails and let out a noise like a bull. Back home, Jacques gave him a handful of change from the jam jar in his room. Guy threw the coins at the wall. "It isn't the same," he screamed. Guy had never spoken to Louis again, as far as Jacques knew.

"I told your boys I'd be fine," Louis said to Jacques. "You have kids that old now?"

"It's been a long time," Jacques said.

"I moved back. My mother's not well. I've been taking care of her and helping out at René's garage." He looked into the ditch. "I guess this will be the end of that."

"We can go back to the house and call René," Jacques's father said. "He has the tow truck."

"Only thing to do, I guess." Louis took a cigarette from a pack in his pocket.

"Let's give it a try," Jacques said. "I'll push. You drive."

He told the boys to stand back with his father. He stepped into the ditch, the muddy water rising over his ankles. He dug his heels in and pushed the bed of the truck as Louis gunned the engine. Mud smacked his face and his shirt.

"That's never going to work," his father called. "We need René. I'll talk to him," he told Louis, who had climbed out of the truck again. "Ask him to give you another chance."

"*Merci,* Monsieur Havre," Louis said, "but I don't think he'll listen."

"He'll listen to me," Jacques's father said. "He was two years behind you, as I remember. *Bon en maths et médiocre en français.*"

"Wait," Jacques said. "There's something else we could try."

"Nothing will work," his father said.

"He's right," Louis said to Jacques.

"Help me get a few of those logs," Jacques told Alexis and Emmanuel. The idea had come out of nowhere, something of him and outside of him, telling him what to do. Alexis and Emmanuel took a log by each end and carried it to the ditch. Jacques dragged another log over the road. His father interjected with "This won't work." Louis tried to roll a log from the stack, then gave up and lit another cigarette. With the help of Alexis and Emmanuel, Jacques wedged the logs under the front tires of the truck. He told Louis to gun the engine again. "Move away with the boys," he said to his father, who did, explaining why the logs would only be buried deeper into the mud and that they needed a tow truck. The engine kicked. Jacques pushed. The bed wobbled and started to rise. He pushed harder, feet slipping. From behind, Alexis and Emmanuel yelled, *"Allez, Papa!"* The tires squealed, the engine whined, and the truck lurched out of the ditch. Jacques fell onto his hands and knees. Louis Nevers yelled his thanks and honked the horn. Alexis and Emmanuel cheered and chased the truck as it drove away.

"He isn't even going straight," Jacques's father said. "He'll end up in another ditch."

"At least it won't be this one," Jacques said.

Back at the cottage, his shoes and socks off and his pants rolled to his calves to keep mud off the floor, Jacques stood in the living room as Alexis and Emmanuel told Jacques's mother and Hélène the story: They'd seen an *"homme tordu"* veer off the road and Jacques had figured out how to get the truck out of the ditch. "The logs were the secret," Alexis said. *"Pauvre* Louis," Jacques's mother said to Henri, who said that Louis hadn't seemed to care at all. "He was probably trying to lose that job with René. He was always lazy at school." He went to light a fire. Hélène told the boys, "That's impressive, but I don't want you

103

wandering off alone, whatever anyone says. And you shouldn't talk to strangers." She lifted her eyebrows at Jacques. They had to get going, Jacques said. He'd go clean up for the drive. "Yes," his father said from the fireplace, "otherwise you'll hit traffic on the *périphérique.*"

In the shower, Jacques watched the mud run off his arms and legs and into the drain, wondering if the pipe would clog. If so, he would hear about it from his father. When they got back to Paris, he would call Guy and tell him that he had a box of vegetables from the garden that he could drop off. Guy would say that he didn't like vegetables, and that Jacques was the one with a family to feed. Jacques would say, All right, then. He closed his eyes and put his face into the stream of water. He would wait for the next time he and Guy had dinner to ask whether the coins had been francs or centimes.

PLUNDER

1999

The night before Herman's treatment, Charlotte dreamed that she was back in the manor in Benneville for the first time in years. She was standing in the parlor, in front of the fireplace, pulling stones from the mantel. Whenever one stone came off, another one appeared in its place. One more and she'd see something. Only one more. "Don't stain your good dress," her mother's voice said. Charlotte looked down and saw that her hands were bleeding.

She woke with a start and held on to Herman until she felt his chest rise with breath. Then she changed out of her nightgown, put on boots and an anorak, and went outside with the bucket that hung by the front door. The house, built of granite and trimmed in the slate blue of Brittany, backed off a cliff facing the Atlantic. A lawn of fennel and thistle ran to a patio with plastic lawn furniture. When Charlotte and Herman had bought the property two years before and moved to Belle-Île from Nantes, they'd taken everything *comme ça:* the tacky lawn furniture, the bad electric, the roof that let in the wind, an attic filled with old shrimping nets, and a cow that grazed in a field out back and seemed to belong to no one.

Charlotte walked down the steps carved into the jagged spill of cliff. The path led to a cove and to a beach, *"notre plage,"* she and Herman called it, although the beach was public, open during the season to sunbathing tourists and to cyclists who parked their bikes on the patio and knocked on the door for directions to Sarah Bernhardt's former home a few miles away. Dawn had broken not long ago, and the fog was just starting to peel off the shore. The Atlantic thrashed, the pale green gone gray with December. Gulls wheeled and shrieked, tilted off-course by the wind. Charlotte checked the horizon but found no clouds. Last night's forecast said today would be clear despite yesterday's storm.

By the time she got to the sand, she'd shaken off the discomfort of the dream. Her anorak flapped and whistled as she walked the tide line, wind sanding her face. Claws of seaweed stretched from the reach of the foam. She picked up what she thought was a piece of sea glass but turned out to be a shard of plastic. Crabs skittered into holes ahead of her steps. At the end of the beach, where the water smashed against rock, she stopped, then made her way back. Halfway up the steps, bucket empty, she checked the horizon again. Yesterday had been so bad that the nine o'clock ferry to Quiberon didn't run on schedule. She would make sure that she and Herman left early and gave themselves plenty of time.

Charlotte first visited the manor when she was five, several years into the war. In her good shoes and best dress, hair braided tight to her shoulders, she stood on the steps one April morning with her mother, who had put on her church hat and drawn seams on the backs of her legs with a charcoal pencil. They were there for Charlotte's first piano lesson with the widow Vouette.

"Remember what I told you," her mother said, as she lifted the lion head knocker. Charlotte must say please and thank you and listen to the widow at the piano. She must keep her voice low and not cross her legs on the bench and sit up straight. She must be *une petite fille adorable.*

"J'arrive," a voice called at the clunk of the knocker. Then the door opened and the widow appeared, holding a basket of laundry. "So this must be Charlotte," she said, looking down.

Charlotte had seen the widow a few times before in Benneville, lined up for rations, in a pew at mass. Up close, she looked soft, as if she were made of melting wax. Her back hunched like a turtle shell, and a hair corkscrewed from her chin. Once, Charlotte's mother had told her, the widow had been *une grande dame,* served by a maid and a gardener at the manor, eating croissants for breakfast each morning, driving around in a silver car, sunning herself in her pergola as she drank a thimbleful of wine. But the war had taken away the widow's croissants and car, the sugar and flour, the wood for the fires, the chocolate, and most of the men in the village, including Charlotte's father. The widow was no longer *grande,* and she didn't have anyone to do her laundry. She still had a piano, though, which made beautiful, rolling music that Charlotte could hear as she and her mother walked by the manor, into the forest. "Do you think I could learn to play the piano?" she had asked her mother one day, and her mother had said, "You've had worse ideas."

That evening Charlotte's mother had gone to the manor to ask the widow if they could make *un petit échange de services.*

"The little one is terribly excited," Charlotte's mother said now. She pushed Charlotte forward. "It is so good of you, *madame,* to teach her."

The widow gave Charlotte's mother the basket of laundry and opened the door wide enough for Charlotte.

"The ironing is on top," she said. "We will see you in an hour."

The door closed behind Charlotte. Ahead, a staircase swept like a dove's wing under a chandelier dripping with crystals. Wedding cake moldings frosted the ceilings. The walls glistened, wine-red with a pattern of blossoms, and through a set of enormous wooden doors, she could see the blare of gold.

"It's like the castle in *La belle et la bête,*" she said.

The widow laughed. "I must be the Beast, then," she said. "Come along, Belle."

Once a week after that, for an hour, Charlotte sat with the widow on the piano bench in the parlor, the walls of which were papered in peacock-blue silk with white fleurs-de-lys. A fireplace, carved with butterflies and grapes, covered one wall. The

109

floors were a glossy checkerboard of pale and dark wood. Sheets draped all of the furniture except for the piano, which gleamed in the light from the window.

At first, the widow showed Charlotte how to do her scales, but on the third lesson, halfway into the A scale, she laid her hand on Charlotte's. "Perhaps I should play for you instead," she said. "If you watch me, you will learn well enough."

So Charlotte kept her hands in her lap and she shifted on the bench when the widow shifted, her bony hands dancing over the keys, music gushing from the piano.

"*C'était une rumba,*" the widow would say, turning the page in the songbook. "And now, for a waltz."

Out the vast doors of the parlor and the vaster doors of the manor, down the drive that resembled spilled milk, in the kitchen of the cottage, Charlotte's mother would be ironing the napkins and sheets on the table, sighing as she pushed the iron over the creases. Before Charlotte was born, she had been a laundress in Benneville, and then she met Charlotte's father, the village *mécanicien* and a true catch. They had a daughter, Madeleine, and they lived next to the garage in a fine house with gas lights and indoor plumbing. When Madeleine was thirteen, Charlotte was born, long after Charlotte's mother had stopped trying for another baby. Charlotte held only scant memories of the time that she lived with her mother and father and Madeleine in the house next to the garage: the smell of petrol on her father's clothes, the flickering candles on the altar at mass as she sat on Madeleine's lap, and the smell of her sister, too, balmy and sweet. They had been, Charlotte's mother said, *une petite famille heureuse* — a happy little family. But the year Charlotte turned two, everything went wrong. First, Madeleine, "like that," ran away with the gypsies. Then the Germans marched into Paris, and Charlotte's father left for the front, where he died of a hole in his stomach. Now he was lying under a slab in the church graveyard, and he couldn't even have a cross, because with his death Charlotte and her mother had become poor. Charlotte's mother had to sell the garage and the house and move to the cottage, where the fireplace coughed out smoke and the water smelled like rotten eggs and came from a well.

On the piano bench, though, Charlotte floated, far, far away from that sad story. The music swept up the air in the room and burst like sunbeams. The widow wasn't an old woman with a hair in her chin. And Charlotte wasn't a girl who had eaten a potato for breakfast, and who had lost a father and sister she could barely remember and who had a mother who sighed all the time and cried herself to sleep at night.

"How is the little one progressing, *madame*?" Charlotte's mother would ask when she returned to the door with the widow's ironing folded over her arm.

"*Merveilleusement,*" the widow said. "I'll see you next week, Charlotte."

Charlotte told her mother that she was learning piano by not touching the keys, and her mother clucked her tongue. "As long as the widow is happy," she said. "She does seem to like you, the old lemon. Maybe she'll leave us a little something when she goes to the angels."

Then they walked back home to the cottage, where the widow's undergarments hung, dripping, over the kitchen sink.

"Bring me anything good?" Herman called from the bedroom when Charlotte came back into the house from the beach, shucking off her boots in the hall.

"*Rien,*" she called back.

She stopped in the WC for a bowl of water and Herman's razor and mirror and put them next to him on the bed. She leaned over to kiss his forehead, careful not to jiggle the mattress.

He touched her nose. "You're an ice cube."

"*Il fait froid,*" she said. "Not stormy like yesterday, though."

She helped him to sit up, hands under his armpits as she used to lift their children. A year before, he would have been up at dawn to take the same walk she'd just returned from, coming back to the house with a perfect fan of a *coquille Saint-Jacques,* a piece of driftwood shaped like an elephant, smooth chunks of sea glass that he claimed came from sunken pirate ships off the coast. He left his collections on the dining room table, saved the best pieces for their grand-children, and tossed the rest back into the ocean during the next morning's walk.

She wedged a pillow behind his back, watching his face for pain. The week before, she had sat with him in an examining room at the hospital in Quiberon, as his doctor held an x-ray to the window and mapped the constellations in Herman's liver and stomach.

"*Je ne comprends pas,*" she had said. "I thought the surgery helped."

"We got most of it," the doctor said. "It

113

only takes one bad cell."

"Take the rest out, then."

"Charlotte," Herman said. "He can't cut out everything."

There had been something new in his face, a calm that looked like resignation.

"We'll keep trying," the doctor said. *"Un autre traitement la semaine prochaine."*

In the elevator, on their way to their car, as the floor numbers lit up one after the other, Charlotte broke the silence.

"I know what you're thinking. You can't give up, Herman."

"I've had a good, long life," he said. "It wouldn't be a tragedy."

She kept her eyes on the numbers. "It would be to me."

One afternoon in late June, two months after Charlotte had started piano, the widow Vouette didn't reply to the knocker when Charlotte and her mother came to the door. The next week, Charlotte stood on the drive with her mother and watched as the widow's son directed the furniture, still covered in sheets, into a truck. A group of men from the village carried the piano down the steps.

"All of that and she didn't leave us a *sou*," Charlotte's mother said. "And you didn't learn a single song."

"Maybe the next people will ask us inside," Charlotte said.

"No one will be able to afford that place." Her mother turned back to the cottage. "*Viens.* Stop looking sad. There's no point in being sad over something you can't have."

All that summer the manor sat empty, the shutters closed like sleeping eyes, as Charlotte and her mother walked by, to the forest. They had to forage for food because the rations kept getting smaller and the line of villagers waiting for bread in Benneville stretched all the way over the square. Charlotte's mother wove branches from the willow trees by the pond into traps to catch rabbits, which she would strip down to the flesh and hang over the sink where she'd once hung the widow's undergarments. They found mushrooms and wild onions, berries and snails. They drank soup made from watercress and dandelion leaves. They weren't the only ones in the forest, and by September the rabbit traps kept coming up empty. Charlotte's mother dug up a square of grass behind the cottage. She let their potato rations grow eyes on the windowsill, then Charlotte helped her to push the potatoes into the soil. "This will feed us in winter," Charlotte's mother said as she hauled another bucket of water from the well and threw it on the plot.

Mornings, her belly tight with hunger, Charlotte would look out her bedroom window to see if the potato plants had crawled out of the earth during the night. She remembered the view of the drive out the window of the parlor, the rise and fall of the widow's music. Nights, she and her mother sat close to the fire, which smelled of horse turds, their faces glistening from the heat, as her mother mended clothes and darned socks and Charlotte practiced her letters on a piece of slate. She was getting ready for school. "You will learn yourself away from me," her mother said once, and Charlotte knew that she was thinking about Madeleine. Her mother's face in the flicker of flames was both sad and angry, as if she were about to cry and also to scream. She did scream a week later when they pulled up the plants in the garden and found scabbed, black potatoes stinking of rot. *"Ils sont malades,"* Charlotte said, trying to calm her mother, but her mother kept screaming and cursing and throwing the potato plants at the forest. Then she went inside and drank the last of the liquor she'd been saving for Christmas and stayed in bed until the next morning.

In October, as they came out of the forest

with baskets of chestnuts, a truck was parked in front of the manor and the shutters were open. "Keep walking," Charlotte's mother said. "I've heard bad things about those people." As they stood in line for their bread that week, Charlotte's mother whispered with the other villagers. The couple who had bought the manor were foreigners, by way of Russia. *Riches,* someone said, very rich. The man owned half of the banks in Paris. The woman tipped the workers at the station twice. An entire train car had been filled with their belongings. They seemed standoffish, spoke little, missed the Saturday market, never seemed to come to Benneville at all, must be living off their caviar eggs and champagne and counting their money. "Like rats in a nest," someone said.

The phone rang while Charlotte was cranking open the windows to let air into the bedroom. It was their daughter, calling from Tours.

"Comment vont les petits?" Charlotte asked — How are the little ones? — before her daughter could say, *"Comment va Papa?"*

When she'd first explained Herman's course of treatment, the children, too, seemed resolved. Then they came to visit

Belle-Île. Dad looked awful, they said. Was this really what he wanted? And was it reasonable to go back and forth to the hospital in Quiberon?

"Bien sûr," Charlotte whispered to them in the kitchen. "And it's our job to help him."

He might make it to Christmas. He might make it to the birth of a grandson expected that spring. He might be well enough again to take a painting lesson at the Pointe des Poulains, which he was planning to do when he found the lump in his neck. As for leaving the island, *"Non,"* Charlotte said. This was their home now. Herman had already said many times that no matter what, he wanted to stay. And it was only a matter of catching a ferry. "It isn't your decision to make," she'd finally told them.

The receiver tucked against her chin, she opened another set of shutters. The baby, their daughter said, had finally cut its first tooth.

"Envoie-nous des photos," Charlotte said. She mouthed their daughter's name to Herman, who held out his hand.

"He's ready for you," she said into the phone, meaning that their daughter was ready for Herman. She was the opening act that smoothed the hitch out of the children's voices and moved them away from questions about cell counts and scans. She gave Herman the phone and went to the kitchen to make him his breakfast as he laughed at something their daughter had said.

Not long after the manor was sold, the black cars of the Germans swarmed into Benneville. Charlotte's mother told Charlotte to stay in the cottage when she went to find kindling, because the forest was no longer safe. Now they took the main road when they walked to the village, and sometimes there were two Gestapo in uniforms near the old mill, and Charlotte's mother had to show her papers. After mass, standing with her mother on the steps of the church, Charlotte caught snatches of the whispers over her head. The nuns at the convent up the main road had been expelled for hiding refugees from Paris. The *épicier* had been arrested for hiding explosives in sacks of flour. The electrical lines had been cut, again. Men were running messages and hiding in the forest. Then, one Sunday, the church doors were locked — the priest had been arrested for hiding the *épicier*'s wife in the sanctuary. A few weeks later, the schoolteacher, Monsieur Havre, was arrested, and the boys' and girls' schools closed.

"Don't worry," her mother said. "You're

smart enough to teach yourself."

A morning soon after, when Charlotte woke up and went to the kitchen, a shiny green chair sat by the fire. "It's made of silk," her mother said, but Charlotte already knew what the material was, and finally, she was touching it, running her hand over the softness as she'd once wanted to run her hand over the walls of the manor.

"You won't believe what happened," her mother said. "The couple in the manor ran off during the night and they left the doors open."

"Partis avec des gitans?" Charlotte said, and her mother said, "Yes, with the gypsies."

Over the next month, objects came and went from the cottage — a grandfather clock, a rug patterned with diamonds, sets of china plates. Nights, Charlotte would wake up to the sound of the front door closing. Voices murmured from downstairs. In the morning, the rug or the clock or the set of plates would be gone, and another item had taken its place. In exchange, she and her mother ate bread again, with butter, and washed their faces with soap. There were books with leather covers for Charlotte to practice reading. Paper and an inkwell and pens so she could practice her letters. Her mother wore stockings instead of drawing on the seams. She smoked cigarettes, and Charlotte drank a morning chocolate instead of chicory flavored with birch syrup.

"You mustn't mention it to anyone." Her mother made a sewing motion over her lips. "It is only borrowing."

"What about when they come back?" Charlotte asked.

"People who run away with the gypsies don't come back," her mother said. "And, anyway, *comme j'ai dit,* it is only borrowing."

For Christmas that year, along with roast beef and tinned peas, there was an almond cake made with real sugar, a tin of pâté for their bread, and a package next to Charlotte's plate when they sat down to eat.

"Ouvre-le," her mother said. "It's from the manor, but this you may keep."

When she unwrapped the present, Charlotte found a wooden doll painted with the face of an old woman in a colorful shawl. "Keep opening," her mother said. Charlotte twisted the halves of the doll open.

Inside was the same woman with fewer lines on her face, inside that doll was a doll with black hair instead of gray, then another, younger one with pink circles for cheeks, then another, even younger, until Charlotte twisted open the last doll to find a baby, the

121

face so tiny that its eyes and mouth blended together, floating in the palm of her hand.

In the kitchen, Charlotte tuned the small radio to the local station to check that the ferry was running on time. The wind was only ten knots and no rain in the forecast. A tanker had sunk the night before in the Bay of Biscay in the storm, but the authorities were confident that there wouldn't be a spill. She opened the valve on the propane tank under the sink and filled the kettle with water. The sand from her walk on the beach crunched under her feet against the slate tile. At first, when she and Herman moved into the house, they swept and vacuumed regularly, but the sand got everywhere — in the bed, in the carpet — and they'd decided *on arrête.* They were going to stop so many unnecessary things: ironing, sitting in traffic, worrying about money. The smell of seaweed and salt instead of gasoline fumes, crushed oyster shells instead of the asphalt of Nantes.

She put a slice of brioche in the toaster. Tea and toast was all Herman could eat. The nausea would have started by the time they got home tonight. Then sores would open on his tongue, and his fingernails would darken. His hands would swell and his legs would shake. Within a few weeks, his eyelashes and eyebrows would have fallen out, and he'd need to wear a wool cap to keep his head warm as he slept.

She waited for the tea to steep. Their first year on the island, they couldn't stop eating. They built seafood towers out of oysters and clams and shrimp, and the difficult-to-pick spiders of the sea. They learned to make *far breton* — creamy prune flan — and crêpes with black flour. They packed picnics of bread and charcuterie, and explored the island on bikes and on foot, visiting the lighthouses, the chapels, the views Monet painted, the Fort Sarah Bernhardt, the menhirs Jeanne and Jean: two clandestine lovers from Druid times, turned into stone. Evenings, they'd drive to Le Palais or Locmaria and sit on a terrace by the ports, drinking *chouchen,* watching the fishermen haul baskets of oysters and sardines into their boats.

She set the tea and toast on a tray. Out the window, on the field behind the house, the cow had wandered into sight and was chewing on a hedge.

Charlotte met Herman in 1959, at a café in Nantes where the girls went to find soldiers from the American military base. She was twenty-one years old, a university student in English, and she had learned not to think about the past. She wrote her mother spottily about her life in Brittany, and she didn't read her mother's replies, simply taking the envelopes from Benneville out of the letterbox in her apartment building and dropping them down the trash chute on her way upstairs. Only in the occasional stubborn dream in which she yanked up floorboards, pulled off stones, smashed holes in the peacock blue walls of the manor, did she return home.

For weeks, she sat at a corner table of the café in a pencil skirt and cardigan, reading *Moby-Dick.* She had an idea of the soldier who would approach her: he would be tall and lanky, as all the Americans seemed to be. He would offer her a cigarette, which she would decline, and then, looking down at her book, he'd say something about Melville. She didn't fully understand the book in her hands, but a man who had read *Moby-Dick,* who was drawn to her because of it, would be someone whom she might like.

Instead, she met Herman, who was shorter than she was and balding on his crown. He didn't even notice her book. After apologizing in surprisingly good French for bumping into her table, he said, "It's better with ice" and pointed to her Coke.

The one doubt that Charlotte had about Herman was that he was too kind, and therefore too simple. He was an air traffic controller on the military base, and when he could get time off, he took her to a patisserie and ordered enough *tartes au citron, mille-feuilles,* and éclairs for four people. His grandmother had been from Marseilles — she had taught him her language — and he seemed to ascribe to the French a goodness that made Charlotte nervous. She told him about growing up in Benneville with her mother and leaving for school on the other side of the country as soon as she could. She told him about trying and failing to find her lost sister, Madeleine.

"My mother says she ran away with the gypsies," she explained, "although you can't believe anything my mother says." This was as close as she got to telling Herman about the manor. But when, a few months after they met, he asked her to marry him, she said, "I need you to see something first."

A week later, her mother ran out of the cottage at the sound of Herman's car.

"Ma petite est revenue," she said. She threw her arms around Charlotte, and left lipstick on Herman's cheeks when she

kissed him. "An American soldier," she said to Charlotte. "Now I understand why you studied English."

Inside, the cottage still smelled like smoke from the fireplace and from the cigarettes Charlotte's mother kept lighting. She talked quickly and constantly, laying out plates of sliced ham and crab salad in iceberg lettuce boats and rice salad she'd made from a box. She had bought herself a small TV, and, as she poured more wine into Herman's glass, she asked him what he thought of this American movie star or that one. Rock Hudson, in particular, she found *magnifique.*

Charlotte listened as her mother chatted on and on with Herman, pretending not to notice that she was flirting with him, and giving them the occasional translation.

"I warned you," she said, after lunch, as she and Herman walked up the drive. "She can't hold her wine."

"She seems happy you're here."

"That wasn't happiness," she said, "that was nervousness. She knows I can't stand her. I try not to be cruel." She took his hand as they passed under the plane trees. "Anyway, she isn't why I brought you here. She's not what I wanted you to see."

Ivy had swallowed all three stories of the

126

manor. The shutters, which had still hung straight when she left for school in Nantes, tipped from their hinges. On the door, a No Trespassing sign hung in place of the lion head knocker.

She led Herman around the side, wading through the knee-high grass to the courtyard and to the set of French doors under the balcony, which had bled trails of rust down the façade.

"Look inside," she said, and she told him what her mother and the other villagers had done during the war.

"They wrecked it," Herman said.

"J'en ai profité," she said, and then to make sure he understood, she repeated it in English. "I profited from it."

Herman looked away from the window. "But you were just a kid."

In English, *but* meant an objection. *Kid* meant "child" and "baby goat." *Just* meant it didn't matter. Charlotte saw that Herman understood enough and couldn't understand completely, and that in that space, she could make a life with him. She knew, too, that he would never make her talk about the manor again, in either language.

Herman was off the phone with their daughter and had started to shave with the bowl of water in his lap and the hand mirror. Charlotte set the tray of tea and toast on the nightstand.

"Did you tell her what the doctor said?" she asked.

"She has enough to worry about. What if the baby's other teeth never come in?"

Charlotte smiled. "We worried about those things too when they were little." She wiped a clot of shaving cream from his chin. "Once you eat, we should go."

He drank a few sips of tea and ate a bite of brioche while she laid out his clothes. She guided his T-shirt over his head, avoiding the chemo port under his collarbone. His jaw had tightened. When they had first made love, he kept asking her if she was all right until she put her hand over his mouth. She had always been harder than he was, she thought, as she helped him out of the bed.

The day the Americans bombed Benneville, the air frizzled with smoke and the crack of gunfire echoed from the forest. Charlotte's mother locked the shutters and bolted the door of the cottage. Charlotte curled up on the floor next to the fireplace with her hands over her ears. Once things quieted, her mother went outside with a shovel and dug a hole in the garden by the well.

"Get the cigarettes," she told Charlotte when she came back inside, "and the stockings."

"Why?" Charlotte said.

"There's no time for questions," her mother said.

They went to and from the house to the hole with the tins of pâté, the stockings and soap, the boxes of cigarettes, the books and the pens, the bottles of champagne and perfume. Her mother got the set of nesting dolls from Charlotte's room. Charlotte looked away as her mother shoveled dirt into the hole. "You'll have other dolls," her mother said.

A few days later, at dawn, the butcher came to the door of the cottage with another man and with Madame Havre, the schoolmaster's wife. *Ma fille. Ma fille,* Charlotte's mother sobbed, as the men put her in the back of the butcher's car. Madame Havre gave Charlotte the biscuit that she had brought, wrapped in a napkin, and she brushed and braided Charlotte's hair. She helped her to pack a sack of clothes, then they walked through the forest to Benneville. She told Charlotte not to cry.

"What if *Maman* doesn't come back?" Charlotte said, and Madame Havre said,

"Non, non." Her mother would return. It would not be as it had been with Charlotte's father and her sister, "or those poor souls who lived in the manor."

"I thought they ran away with the gypsies," Charlotte said.

Madame Havre shook her head. The couple, she said, had been taken away by the Germans. They had stopped in the clearing where Charlotte and her mother used to pick dandelion greens, and Charlotte felt as if the world were tilting — the trees against the sky, the ground under her feet — as Madame Havre told her what had really happened. Her mother had done something wrong, and so had many people. They had taken all of the furniture and objets d'art out of the manor and traded them on the black market. Then they smashed open the walls and pulled up the floorboards, looking for money.

"And there was none to find," Madame Havre said.

Charlotte spent two nights in the schoolmaster's house, helping Madame Havre with her twin sons, Jacques and Guy. Outside, Benneville was broken and smoldering. Monsieur Havre lay in bed with bandages on his head and splints on his legs. Madame Havre fed him tisane from a spoon, and at night she brushed Charlotte's hair and gave her a bowl of warm goat's milk with honey. She said that it was nice to have a girl around, and Charlotte wondered, guiltily, if the Havres would let her stay if indeed her mother didn't come back.

But her mother did return, a week later. She knocked softly on the door and said, *"Où est ma fille?"* Where is my daughter? Charlotte was holding baby Guy on her lap at the table, and when her mother stepped into the kitchen, Charlotte saw that her head was shaved so it looked like an onion bulb, and her dress was ripped at the shoulder. "I'm here, *Maman,*" she said. On their way out of Benneville, people Charlotte knew and didn't know shouted and hissed at Charlotte's mother. From the *terrasse* of the café, the *garçon* growled up a mass of phlegm that quivered like jelly on her mother's eyelid. Her mother blinked it away. She squeezed Charlotte's hand.

"Everyone will forget," she said. "And what choice did we have? We were starving."

As the train station fell behind them and the forest rose ahead, Charlotte tried to remember that feeling of hunger deep in her belly, that feeling that, she knew, was not the feeling of starving.

Later, as her mother slept, she went out the back door of the cottage. She found the place near the well where her mother had made the hole, and she dug out the dirt with her fingers. She cleaned the old-woman doll with the hem of her nightgown and pushed back the dirt. She walked up the drive to the manor and squeezed through a glass door with a broken pane. Shards of tile glowed on the floor. The walls and ceiling had been knocked clean away, leaving only beams and furring. She continued on down the hacked-up hallway, around chunks of plaster, an island of bricks. The chandelier, stripped of its crystals, hung like a plucked vine over the gap-toothed staircase. Everywhere, holes riddled the floors. The air swarmed with dust. In the parlor, a heap of baseboards lay where the piano had stood. Charlotte went to the window and put the nesting dolls on the sill, facing the drive.

She pulled over twice on the drive to Le Palais because Herman felt sick, once at the edge of a moor, and once in the parking lot of an abandoned sardine cannery, where she helped him out of the car to throw up the tea and toast.

"It's the twists in the road," she said, her hand on his back as he retched.

"And later on the ferry, it will be the waves." He stayed crouched with his hands on his knees. "What will it be tonight? And tomorrow?"

Don't be bitter, she wanted to say, that isn't like you.

"I'll go slower," she said. She helped him upright.

She was in line for the ferry at eight thirty. The ocean looked calm, the horizon cloudless. Herman had fallen asleep before they got to Le Palais and was snoring now, a slow, rattling sound. When his head slipped on the window, Charlotte pushed it back gently against the seat. A car drove into the space behind.

At a quarter to nine, the ferry from Quiberon still hadn't docked to let off passengers, at ten to nine neither. Charlotte started to worry. Herman sighed in his sleep. He looked as pale and thin as paper, curled up against the car door. At nine, when still no ferry had appeared, she turned off the engine and lowered the window for Herman.

She walked down the aisle formed by waiting cars to the ferry building. From the doors, she sensed a commotion. Workers in hooded slickers were rushing around with walkie-talkies. Passengers waited, smoking,

133

talking, looking distressed. A group of them stood under a television that had been tuned to the news.

"*Quel désastre,*" someone said.

The tanker that had sunk in the Bay of Biscay the night before had cracked in two and was spilling "*des milliers de tonnes de pétrole*" into the bay.

"Is that why the ferry is late?" Charlotte asked a man.

"*Je suppose,*" the man said. "*Quel merdier.* And the oil is on its way here."

Behind the ticket desk, a woman with acne-pitted cheeks was watching the television through the glass. She slid back the window without looking at Charlotte.

"Will the ferry make it here soon?" Charlotte asked.

The woman glanced at her and then looked back at the television. The port in Quiberon was a mess, she said. "*Comme vous pouvez imaginer, madame.*"

"But when will it arrive?"

The woman looked at her coldly. "*Vous n'êtes pas d'ici, n'est-ce pas?*"

"*Non,*" Charlotte said. "What does that matter?"

"If you were from here, you would understand what this spill means. And you would be less worried about a late ferry."

She shut the window. People had lined up behind Charlotte. A baby was crying. *"Catastrophe écologique,"* the television said. Charlotte tapped on the window. The woman was talking to a man in a uniform with stripes on the shoulders who had come into the office. Charlotte felt a rise of the energy she'd woken up with from the dream, a force beyond her control, making her pull off the stones. She tapped on the window again. *"Mon mari est malade,"* she said, then repeated it louder.

The woman shook her head, but the man leaned around her and opened the window.

"Je peux vous aider, madame?" he said.

"My husband is ill," Charlotte repeated. Her head was spinning. "We need to get to Quiberon."

"If there is no ferry, there is no ferry, you see," the man said. "There is little that we can do."

"But will it come?"

"You say your husband is ill. Shall I get help? Is this an emergency?"

"Non," Charlotte said, her head spinning faster. "Not an emergency."

"We can help you move your car out of the line if you don't want to wait."

"Charlotte," a voice said from behind her. "What are you doing?"

135

When she turned around, she saw a dying man. He was out of breath, and his skin had a strange, clammy hue. His bald head gleamed in the fluorescent lights, his eyes sank in their sockets. Behind him, people waited in line, looked at the television, got coffees from the machines against the walls, ashed their cigarettes. They pulled stray threads from their sweaters, chewed gum, breathed, swallowed. This man, he was dying. *Il meurt,* she thought.

"There was an oil spill in the bay," she told Herman. "It's holding up the ferry." She started to cry.

"We'll wait," Herman said. "Come back to the car, sweetheart."

He took her arm, but she didn't move.

"It's all right," she said. "We can turn around if you want to."

It took a half hour to move the car out of the line with the help of the ferry workers. When they got back home, Herman said, "Let's go to the beach," but his legs wobbled on the first step down the cliff. Charlotte helped him over to the patio and into one of the plastic lawn chairs. She went inside for a blanket and made two cups of tea. Through the window, the cow had drifted out of view again. As the tea steeped, she turned on the radio. A sheen had appeared on the surface of the bay near the place where the tanker had sunk.

Outside, she laid the blanket on Herman's legs and gave him his cup of tea.

"Tiens," she said. "Careful, it's hot."

She sat down next to him and took his hand. Tomorrow, at dawn, when she went down the steps, she'd find black sand, rocks as slick as rubber, ashy foam on the ocean, and gulls that struggled to open their wings. Now, though, there was the silver water, the curtains of cliffs, the pale spread of the beach, and the sun, bright and clueless, in the middle of the sky.

NOTHING OF CONSEQUENCE

1975

They came to Madagascar — women, all educators — to train a group of French teachers from around the island. They were housed in the living quarters of an abandoned coconut plantation and conducted their classes in warehouses still dusty with copra. By the second week, the red soil had colored their soles, and the sun, their faces. Though in the classroom they were as rigorous as they were back home, their minds drifted. Lessons on the imperfect, discussions of Orientalism, were interrupted by thoughts of what would be served for lunch or whether a driver might be hired for an excursion to the rain forest. They returned to themselves when a student raised a hand.

One man in particular impressed the women from the start because he never made an error in construction or conjugation, and he listened to their explanations with a critical tilt to his head. Unlike the other students, who wrote in pencil, Rado Koto took notes with a fountain pen. He was young, in his twenties, but he walked in his youthful body as if borrowing it on the way to an older one. A lycée teacher in the capital, he intended to live one day in France and pursue *"sa poésie."*

At the first night's dinner, after punch coco and before fish curry, Rado sat down next to Bernadette, who, since the orientation in Paris, had barely cracked a smile or revealed anything about herself except that her husband had been dead a year and that she found Colette underrated. She was the most taciturn and the least attractive among them. The boldness of her blunt chin and large mouth might have made for pretty ugliness during her youth but in late middle age made her look plain. She wore collared shirts, buttoned just below her clavicle, the sleeves rolled over her elbows. Judging by the measure of her chignon, her hair would fall to her shoulders.

As Bernadette spoke to Rado, she fiddled with the corner of her napkin. Now and again she laughed, which the women had never heard her do, not even that afternoon when they'd attended a performance of a dance troupe in the nearby village and were all brought onstage for a lesson. Rado laughed with her. The solitary line that marked his brow deepened, and his teeth showed, as they didn't in the classroom. Neither of them got up to help bring the dishes out from the kitchen until, the plates being cleared, Bernadette looked around apologetically and announced that she and Rado would fetch the pudding. The next evening, and the next, Bernadette and Rado seemed always to be leaving for the kitchen or talking over their untouched food. Their discussions could be overheard in snatches: Rimbaud's Catholicism, the lyrics of Prévert, nothing to raise suspicion in the director, hunched over his plate at the other end of the table, necktie tucked into his shirt front. But the women interpreted what he ignored. In the communal bathroom, on the path to meals, and evenings, over tisanes, Bernadette and Rado became the subject of hushed conversation.

The coconut, he told her, as she followed him into the plantation, could travel for hundreds of miles on the ocean, even washing up on the shores of Antarctica and Ireland.

"Vraiment?" she asked.

140

He smiled. "There is no fooling you, is there?"

"Maybe if you were a botanist. Instead of a poet."

At dinner, the third night, he had shown her his notebooks of verse, which he hoped to publish in France, since on the island there was no press. She recognized the force of will it must have taken for him to go to university, having grown up in a one-room house with eight brothers and sisters, fated to work in the nickel mines or on vanilla plantations. But his writing seemed to her to have no heart, all corroded tin roofs under the cruel sun, waves that stabbed, the bitterness of tree frogs. Although he'd grown up poor, he hadn't known suffering. Despite the beauty in his lines, this showed.

"I used to hide in the coconut fronds when I was supposed to be doing my chores," he said.

"You would have done better living in France. Oaks and pines give good cover."

"You did that too?"

"Don't all children? I spent half my time off the ground as a girl."

Rado stopped to pull a frond blade from the heel of his sandal. She imagined him shirtless and barefoot while she sat between her parents in the church of Benneville, her baby sister, Charlotte, on her lap, trying to keep still as the priest gave his warnings about sin and damnation. But no, she realized, calculating the difference in their ages, that wasn't right. When Rado was a boy, she was carrying babies and groceries up the steps of her apartment building in Paris. When Rado's voice was starting to change, she was years into her fine, dull marriage, sitting at her kitchen table with a stack of papers to grade, ignorant of the affair her husband had recently ended.

Only Bernadette's roommate protested the rumors. "Who knows what's going on in your room when you aren't there," one woman said, and the roommate said, "Reading." She saw what the others didn't see: Bernadette tossed in her sleep; she changed into her nightgown in the bathroom and slept with the sheets pulled up to her chin. If Bernadette got up at night, it was only to go down the hall to the bathroom. She never took long. And was it so terrible, anyway, that Bernadette had something she looked forward to in the morning, something that made her check her face in the mirror? The mirror was small and low on the wall, the light poor, and as the roommate walked into the room, Bernadette was bent toward the glass, cupping her cheeks as one might those of a child. This the roommate didn't mention, but a few days later, when one of the women cornered her to let her know that Bernadette was now smoking Rado's cigarettes, the roommate said she was starting to be reminded of *The Crucible*.

"I am becoming the subject of gossip," Bernadette told Rado.

He laughed and took her hand to help her over a fallen tree, an unnecessary gesture that closed her throat. She could smell his body through his clothes: a stiff white shirt, a pair of creased pants, the apparel of a schoolboy. If she had been another kind of woman, she would have wanted to take him to the shops on the avenue Montaigne to pick out scarves and sweaters.

"It's the same for me," he said. "When I go back to my village, the women in the market spread rumors about me. A chorus of hoopoe birds." He stopped so that she could move ahead on the path. *"Les huppes ici sont jalouses de toi."*

"What do I have to envy?" The hope in her voice made her cringe.

"A university professorship."

"Not everyone wants that. And it's only part-time."

He understood nothing of the *Éducation nationale.* She had told him that she taught at a lycée and a course in the continuing studies department of the university, so he imagined her to be a professor. She saw it happen the first night, the way his eyes stopped roaming. She didn't correct him.

The ground turned from grass to sand. Ahead was the ocean.

"The whales are migrating," Rado said. "You can see them from here."

"Really," she said flatly, and then laughed. "I'm sorry. Animals have never been my thing."

"We will never own a dog together, then."

Although she knew he was teasing, she felt blood rush to her face, one of the symptoms her husband complained about in the early stage of his illness. Flushing. Shortness of breath. Dizziness. Pain near the heart. Was that why he was brought back to his mistress in those days? Why he disclosed the affair? "I've always loved only you," he told her from the hospital bed, and she hadn't said, "I've only loved one man, and he was a boy, a long time before you." Instead, she kissed his pale lips and said, *"Je te pardonne."*

Rado was telling her about the song of the indri lemur, which sounded like that of a humpback. "A whale in a tree," he said, and she knew that he wished he had his notebook. She felt irritated.

"I saw a snake this morning on the reef," she said.

He lowered his hands — he had been charting the course of an invisible lemur through the canopy above — and fumbled in his shirt pocket for his cigarettes. "You're lucky," he said. "You wouldn't want a bite from one of those."

"Do you believe in omens?" she said.

"No," he said. *"Ni aux tabous."*

The boy that she'd loved was named Gabriel. He lived with his parents on a small farm outside of Benneville. *Les Italiens,* the neighbors called them. She met him the spring she turned fourteen. She had been going to the forest after school to avoid heading home to her mother's judgments over her hair not being right, the ink stain on the hem of her skirt, her unkempt nails, her general lack of elegance. Meanwhile, Charlotte, with her big eyes and cheeks, was perfect, like the dessert she'd been named for: creamy and sweet and plump. And she didn't talk, so she couldn't talk back.

One afternoon, she turned down the trail that led to the stone walls of the old Léger estate and saw a boy jimmying open the lock on the gate with a pocketknife.

"Ne t'inquiète pas," she said when he turned around. "I haven't seen anything." She assumed from the bag over his shoulder that he was poaching rabbits. He had a pale, thin face with full lips, and bushy hair that sprouted from under a cap. He pushed open the gate and took off the cap, gesturing with it for her to pass by.

"It's ten o'clock," he said, in broken French. "The widow and her maid have gone to mass and the gardens are open to visitors."

They met there every afternoon for the next two weeks. They sat in the pergola, under the lacy umbrella of wisteria that kept out a summer rain. They put ivy crowns on the heads of the muses, and tried to hit the chimneys with burrs from the chestnut tree. Gabriel took her to the back wall of the manor and showed her fossils in the stone. She leaned in and licked the curl of a shell, and he did the same.

The third week, he kissed her as they drank from the fountain. By June, they were stripping off their clothes before they'd got through the gate. There was a soft patch of grass near the topiary. After, they'd lie curled up together. He whispered to her in

Italian, and she imagined what he must be saying. When they heard the clunking sound of the widow's car, they grabbed their clothes and ran into the forest.

Some of the women mentioned the situation, as they called it, to their husbands when they phoned home from the director's office, left to them after he'd gone to bed. His quarters were on the floor above, and as they talked through the crackle of static, the women thought of the director and kept their voices down for fear that he might be listening. The husbands barely reacted. Twenty years earlier, upon hearing about Bernadette, the husbands might have worried about their own marriages. Twenty years earlier, at the airport in Paris or Lyon, the husbands would have kissed their wives longer. A few of the women became angry upon hanging up. Bernadette might have it right. What if they found a student of their own? Broke rules in all directions. Right there in the classroom, against the map of Europe, or, like Bernadette, on the beach, where they supposed she and Rado went.

From where Bernadette stood with Rado, the reef looked smooth as a rug, but up close it was a web of crags and holes. The

147

water was layered, a crust of cold and warmth below, the reverse of the students, whose smiles hid gentle disdain. Four-Eyes, Old Chicken, Good Girl. Rado had told her the nicknames that the students coined for their teachers. Back home, Bernadette had friends like the women, friends who held her hand at her husband's funeral, called daily in the following weeks, took her to weekend houses in Normandy, and, after a decent interval for her to grieve, would want to invite her to dinner with divorced and widowed men. Friends who worried about her, about the way she picked up and ran off, as they called it, giving them notice only a week before.

Earlier, her roommate had asked her for the third time if she'd like to go swimming, and Bernadette agreed, not wanting to tip into rudeness. Also, this was something to fill the morning until Rado was free. Bernadette went right into the water, while the roommate, winded from the walk, said she would rest first with her book. When Bernadette kicked to the surface, having seen the snake coiled in a crevice, the roommate raised her eyes.

Looking down, Bernadette saw that in her escape, the knot of her bathing suit had come undone. She was naked to the waist.

"Why not?" the roommate called, and untied her own halter. Bernadette covered herself back up with a quick knot to her bathing suit straps.

"It was an accident," she told her roommate, "but yes, why not?"

Later, back at the compound, before they parted ways, the roommate said, "Do you really care for him?" Though her voice was hard, her face wasn't, and it occurred to Bernadette now, as Rado lit her cigarette, that the roommate might not have been fishing at all but instead giving a warning.

If Bernadette hadn't held herself apart, hadn't taken on airs, the women might have felt sorry for her. Rado, in the end, would move on. He was interested only in Bernadette's connection to the university system, though his hope was false, since she was, after all, a *vacataire,* not a real professor. He would have been better off with the one who came from Lille and ran a feminist press and had friends in the right places. Or with the prettiest one, whose smooth skin and tight figure they all envied. If Bernadette and Rado ended up together, since these things sometimes happened (there was talk of the friend of a friend who after a stint with a medical nonprofit married a man from the Congo), Rado would expect Bernadette to wait on him like a slave. Seen in this light, they were victimizing each other.

They sat down on the beach. "Show me where you're from," Rado said.

Bernadette told him the name, drew a map of France in the sand with her finger and pointed to the north. "It wasn't much of a village to start with and it was destroyed during the war."

"Your family remains there?"

"I don't know. I haven't been back since I was a girl." She smoothed out the map. "Some families are meant to be left. Besides, Paris is nicer."

"I've always wanted to see Paris," Rado said. "The grave of Baudelaire."

Was that the beginning? The opening? Would he bring up not having enough for a ticket? Could she lend him the money? Was that how this kind of thing went? In the hospital, she'd interrupted her husband's deathbed confession and said, "Stop talking." If only he had told her years earlier, when she was a young woman, maybe she would have left him, or maybe she would have stayed. Maybe she would have had her own affair. She didn't know. He had robbed her of the choice.

"My apartment is in that *quartier*," she said, and then wished she hadn't.

Rado looked up at a coconut tree. *"Tu en veux?"*

She nodded. And then he was gone. Feet flat on the trunk, he climbed toward the fronds. His heels looked tender against the leathered trunk. She felt a twinge of pity. Here, or in France, he would rise to become head of a school district. He would wear bow ties.

A coconut thumped down beside her. "Too close?" Rado called.

She picked up the coconut and handed it to him when, breathing heavily, he returned to the ground. "Why are your eyes full?" he said.

"You make me think of someone."

"Ton mari?"

"No," she said. "He was afraid of heights."

Then the moment was gone. He was Rado again, and she was this woman in the sand, not that girl in the forest.

After husking the coconut, Rado slammed the point of a pocketknife into its eyes. He pressed the coconut to Bernadette's mouth, and the water spilled over her chin. She pushed the coconut away. He kissed her neck.

"Don't," she said.

He put the coconut to his own mouth and drank.

"I'm sorry," he said when he was done. "It's too soon for you. My grandfather has been gone ten years, and still my grand-mother can't look at his picture without weeping."

"It's not that," she said. "I'm not thirsty."

"So let's not drink." He threw the coconut down the beach and leaned in to her again. Her heart was thumping. She unbuttoned her shirt.

The morning that Gabriel didn't arrive, she sat in the pergola until she heard the sound of the widow's car. She walked the logging road to the main road, through Benneville, to Gabriel's farm. He was in a field with his father, digging potatoes. He looked up at her and then went back to jamming his spade into the dirt, but not before she saw the bruise on his neck. She stood on the road, watching him and his father dig. When she opened the door to her house, her father yanked her into the kitchen. He said that she was no better than a *putain.* He'd talked to the boy's father, and that was the end of that. Her mother was sobbing at the table. "How could you do this to us," she cried, as Charlotte called from her crib in the other room. A week later, the women at the market said that the Italians who sold the chickens had moved away. They owed thousands of francs to the bank for their farm, apparently. What could you expect from Italians? They were all a bunch of dirty cheaters.

Bernadette and Rado were seen walking back from the beach, without bags or towels, her hair unattached, her hand in his. That evening, at dinner, the women couldn't look down the table without imagining that elegant mouth on Bernadette's. Rado, too big for his chair, seemed to them dangerous and fragile. In Bernadette, as she passed the bowl of salad and salted her fish, the women watched for some sign of regret, but she was straight-shouldered and quiet, her hair back in its chignon. Each of the women, for her own reasons, was resolute. They went to bed having decided what they must do.

The next morning as Bernadette left class, the director called her into his office. When he was done talking, Bernadette said, "You patronize him. Is it his youth or his color?"

"It is the abuse of power," the director said. "You're his teacher."

"We did nothing wrong," she said. That was all she would give him. She had decided so at dinner the previous night as she and Rado were bathed in sidelong stares. Or maybe the preparation started earlier, when she walked away from her roommate without answering the woman's question.

"I'll go," she said. "Leave him be."

Outside, she passed students reading under a baobab tree, playing a game of checkers on the grass. She thought of the papers being stacked and blackboards being wiped behind the cloudy classroom windows. What would they talk about now? She walked, head up, gaze straight, just as she'd walked the road out of Benneville one night, pockets filled with money from the till in her father's garage. She followed the main road until her feet hurt, to the convent that stood by the river, where she gave the name Bernadette Léger. She spent seven months scrubbing floors and washing habits, praying for the redemption of her soul. Her water broke in the chapel. She closed her eyes from the first push, and squeezed them tighter when the pain was over and the room filled with the cries of what, a nun told her later, had been a boy.

She sat in her room by the window, bags packed, and watched the sky drift down into

154

the trees. She could still feel the softness of Rado's hand as they'd walked back from the beach. When he started to let go as the trees thinned for the buildings, she held on tighter. For the first time since his death, she felt tenderness for her husband.

"You shouldn't have come," she said after opening the door to Rado's knock.

"They're too busy toasting their victory to notice." He sat on the edge of the bed. "I know you took the blame. Your roommate told me."

"She saw it coming."

"What will happen to you?"

"Nothing of consequence."

"You threw yourself on the sword," he said. "Why?"

It was the first time he'd asked a real question about her, and for a moment she believed that they were what he seemed to think they were: tragic lovers. Then he smiled and she wasn't sure what he thought.

"I leave that to you," she said.

When his first book was published in France, some of the women sought it out and others stumbled upon it. He was the only writer in the history of the island to win such a prestigious award. They flipped through the pages in bookstores, in bed, on the couch, looking for something they recognized. They didn't know where truth ended and poetry began. They didn't know if Rado climbed a tree to pick a coconut or if Bernadette punctured the eyes with her thumbs. Did she undress him like a mother? Did a thicket of palm fronds grow over the sky? They didn't know if the ocean claimed the empty shell, which floated around the Horn of Africa and past the icebergs of the north. They didn't know if the coconut still traveled, studded with barnacles and bleached by salt. There was so much they didn't know.

Years later, she saw a poster with his photograph as she walked with her granddaughter back from the Jardin des Tuileries. *Shakespeare and Company présente le deuxième livre de Rado Koto.* The next night, she stood in the back of a crowded room at the bookstore, propped on her cane. Rado looked sickly at the podium, his jaw gaunt and his eyes too deep as he read his poems, which were different from those of his first book, similar to the ones he'd once shown her in his notebook. Beautiful but hard, she thought, then with frustration and now, she supposed, with disappointment.

The reading over, he sat with his American

translator, signing the French edition as his translator signed the English. She handed him the copy of his book.

"Je le dédie à qui, madame?" he said, after glancing up at her.

"To Madeleine," she said.

HALF LIFE

One September evening, when Kate came
home from her job at the Grenoble Museum
of Art, there he stood in the garden, next to
the boxwood hedge. He was long, preda-
tory: a wolf, she thought at first, illogically,
but no, that was a dog. His right front leg
had a hole like a knot in a tree, and his fur
resembled an old shag rug. One of his eyes
was partially closed; he seemed to be sizing
Kate up. She stood on the path, satchel in
hand, and wondered if the dog might be
rabid. "Shoo," she said, then, *"Va-t'en!"* In
response, the dog limped over the grass to
the bench by the door and, after turning
three times, curled up underneath. He was
still there the next morning, even though
Kate had propped open the gate. She left
him a bowl of water, and added a plate of
steak haché the next night. By the third day,
she'd accepted that the dog was not going

to budge.

"He's giving me the stink-eye," her house-mate, Georgia, said. They were having breakfast in their small backyard, at the picnic bench that Kate had scavenged from one of Grenoble's *antiquaire* shops. When they'd come outside, the dog limped from under the bench and lay in the grass at Kate's feet.

"I don't think it does that on purpose. There's something wrong with its eye."

"Among other things." Georgia sucked an udon noodle through her cupped tongue. She'd heated up leftover Japanese and was cross-legged on a broken chair, her robe parted to show a strip of crotch. "The fucked-up dog of a fucked-up human."

A week before the dog appeared, the *police municipale* had dispersed a homeless en-campment on the Bastille, the fortified hill behind the house that Georgia and Kate rented. The homeless migrated to Grenoble during the summer, playing guitars and fiddles on street corners, mangy dogs like this one often sleeping nearby. They were not gypsies. They were Europeans on foot who roamed the EU and ended up in Spain or Portugal for the winter. Kate and Georgia had surmised that the dog had been sepa-rated from its owner and wandered down the hill, into their yard, to find food.

"I certainly can't keep him," Kate said. "My one experience with a pet was a disaster. A hamster. It escaped its cage. The cleaning lady thought it was a mouse, and she whacked it with a broom."

It was Kate who had neglected the latch on the cage door. The hamster frothed at the mouth and staggered in its wheel for two days. Her mother said maybe the hamster only had a concussion and would recover. "How could you do that to her?" her father had yelled at her mother when he returned home from his business trip. "Can't you take care of anything?" He told Kate that he would get her another hamster and that she should go up to her room. As she walked up the stairs, Kate heard him ask her mother for a plastic bag and a hammer.

"Maybe he's the reincarnation of that hamster." Georgia sucked up another noodle. "Your second chance."

"I didn't kill the hamster," Kate said. "I don't need another chance." Georgia might be vulgar and not perfectly educated, but she displayed an innate intelligence. In her early thirties, like Kate, she worked at the English bookstore in the city, which catered to the University of Grenoble's large student

160

population from the British Isles and the United States, young people drawn to the city mostly for its proximity to the Alps and the good skiing. She had a wild, free-ranging sex life, the details of which she enjoyed sharing at breakfast after spending the night elsewhere. She said that monogamy was an institution meant to keep women down and that she had an elevated level of testosterone manifested by her ring fingers being longer than her middle fingers. Currently she was in an S&M relationship with a bartender at Le Couche Tard who made sculptures out of bicycle rims. Although Georgia was endlessly more interesting than Kate on the sexual front, Kate knew that her bohemian sparkle hid a shadow of desperation. It was the greatest act of intimacy to share a bathroom, Kate thought sometimes, and it was only after a few weeks of living with Georgia that she'd noticed the acidic smell in the bathroom near the bidet and connected it with the empty carton of Carte d'Or ice cream in the kitchen trash can or the *tarte au citron* that Georgia had suggested they eat straight from the box while watching a movie. Kate now understood Georgia's Modigliani body, which she'd claimed to keep trim through hot yoga and *la gymnastique*. Although she liked Georgia,

Kate would not want to be her for anything, and she was not thrilled that in certain ways — age, unmarried status, job status, and housing situation — she was.

"Have you told Monsieur Havre about the dog yet?" Georgia said. She referred to Kate's boyfriend, Alexis, by his surname, because, as she put it, he was square as a napkin. "You'll make him nervous. He'll think you want a baby. First the dog, then the baby."

"I'm not having kids. Alexis knows that. And the dog will be gone by the time he gets here. I'll put up signs." At Kate's feet, the dog let out one of its high-pitched sighs.

That afternoon, Kate stood in the phone booth outside the museum for her weekly phone call with Alexis. They had a routine well established, just as they'd had when Alexis lived in Grenoble. A morning email, a nightly email, and the weekly call. Kate had woken up that morning to a description of the drive Alexis made back from Lapland to Stockholm, where he was spending a year doing a postdoctorate. He would return to Grenoble to visit her in three weeks.

"Bonjour, mon chou," he said through the crinkle of static. *"Tu as toujours le chien?"*

"Salut," she said. "Dog still around. Did

you find anything?"

"*Peut-être,* but we have to wait for the soil sample results to be sure."

Alexis's PhD at the University of Grenoble had focused on ionizing radiation; for his postdoctoral study, he was creating a map of the fallout left by the Chernobyl cloud as it had traveled across Western Europe, from Ukraine to the Atlantic Ocean. On their first date, two years before, at a couscous restaurant in the *quartier arabe,* he'd described how the cloud skimmed mountaintops and rained onto fields in Sweden, Switzerland, and even Scotland, where sheep registered radiation in their milk. Mushrooms in a certain region of Austria should be avoided, along with the wild boar of the Vosges. "There are areas right near here," he said, in the Parc national des Écrins. His blond hair shagged around his clean-shaven face, and his eyes looked smart and aware behind his glasses. He was both passionate and calm. Kate had been on too many dates both in Grenoble and back home in the U.S. with men who leaned over the table to convince her of their fabulousness. Alexis stopped himself before he went on too long, shrugged, and said, "Anyway, what about you?"

Over the next year and a half, before he

left for his postdoc, one night together a week became three. A good-night phone call every other day became a good-night phone call every day. After six months, as they sat in the sculpture garden of the museum, where Kate managed the gift shop, Alexis said, *Je t'aime,* and Kate said it back. Alexis told her that she was the first woman he'd actually loved — "because you don't have expectations, except that we shouldn't cheat on each other."

The women he'd dated before, he said, kept giving him ultimatums. They wanted him to say he loved them within the first few months. They wanted to move in together, to get engaged, to get pregnant before they turned thirty.

"How can you know if you love someone when you're under that kind of pressure?" he said.

Kate understood. Although the light by which she saw many things differed from his — was fuzzier, rosier maybe, less scientific — she believed that relationships were better navigated with boundaries, and that this did not, as one boyfriend had put it, make her "heartless" and "detached." It made her realistic.

Neither of them wanted to get married or become parents. Alexis said he'd decided a long time ago that the world was too messed up for children. Kate explained that watching her parents remarry five times between the two of them, and accumulating all those stepsiblings whom she barely knew, had made her think that not getting married might be the way to ensure that a relationship worked. "Plus," she said, "I like my space. As you do." She could read on the couch with her feet in Alexis's lap one night while he watched *le foot,* and be home in her own bed the next.

At five, she shut the glass doors to the gift shop, locked up the display cases, secured the bronze Degas dancer earrings, aligned the postcards, refolded a Van Gogh sunflower scarf on a table, and headed through the *antiquités* collection toward the Espace Atelier. The guards were checking the hallways for lagging visitors. She said *bonjour* and *salut,* and stopped to whisper-chat with the one in the Art Moderne wing, who was doing a study of Matisse's *Intérieur aux aubergines* in a sketchbook, another aspiring artist of which, it seemed, the world and this museum were full.

"I'll be quick," she assured him about her visit to the art studio.

"You can spend the night in there if you

165

like," he said. "There are no security cameras."

Kate wondered by the way he was looking at her whether he meant she could spend the night there with him. This must happen to Alexis all the time at the University of Stockholm, a treasury, she supposed, of beautiful students. The thought made her feel queasy.

"I have to make a sign about a dog," she said bluntly, and continued down the hall.

The *atelier* lay at the end of the contemporary wing with a view of the *jardin de sculptures,* where caterers were setting up tables under the steel wings of a Calder for yet another wedding reception. The *atelier* hosted school groups every Tuesday morning, and the glue sticks were ready on the tables, the words *Bienvenue dans le Monde de Picasso* written on the whiteboard. Kate sat in one of the small chairs and, for the next hour, made fliers out of lime green and peacock blue paper, gluing the photographs of the dog that she'd photocopied on her lunch break. By six, when a guard came by for a final sweep, she'd finished ten identical collages with the dog at the center, looking somewhat corpse-like, and the words *CHIEN PERDU* cut from *Le Dauphiné Libéré* staggered across the top.

"Merveilleux," Georgia said of the fliers that evening. Kate had come home to find her and her boyfriend, Oliver, sharing a bottle of vodka on the couch, under a poster of Georges de La Tour's Saint Jérôme being flagellated by angels. The house, one of a few stand-alones in the neighborhood, had a nice view of the Isère River, which ran by the Bastille, but the foundation, as in most of the homes in the *quartier italien,* was steeped in floodwater, leaving the air musty and damp. The plaster cracked and fell in chunks from the walls, so Kate had masked the holes with posters from the museum gift shop. The living room — a Grecian urn here, a nude by Ingres there — provided a visual crash course in Western art history.

"Thanks," Kate said.

"No, I mean it."

"Très cubiste," Oliver said.

"That's what I was going for."

"We'll help you put them up." Georgia poked Oliver on the temple. "Come on. It'll be fun."

"Whatever you want, chicken," Oliver said. For an unpleasant moment, Kate saw Georgia on the floor of his apartment, blindfolded and handcuffed to his radiator as he dripped candle wax on her inner thighs, a moment that Georgia had told

167

Kate gave her an orgasm so intense she almost passed out.

"Great," Kate said, and went upstairs to change. She didn't like Oliver, and not only for the way he'd made fun of her fliers. She'd dated guys like him: one of them gave her chlamydia. He had dirty-looking hair, tattoos up his neck, and the casual, dangerous gaze of someone who slept around. He cultivated his working-class London accent and ran with a set of Grenoble hipsters from small European countries who self-published chapbooks of Oulipo poetry, dressed up as clowns for readings, held Ping-Pong tournaments, and played the accordion ironically.

They went out into the night, over the bridge, Georgia staggering, Oliver loping, Kate following with the posters. The smell of pizza from the *quais* mixed with the smell of sewers — Grenoble's perfume. Kate found blank areas of wall between the kebab restaurants, pharmacies, and nightclubs where she could tape the posters. Georgia and Oliver ran into one of their friends almost immediately and Kate said she'd meet up with them at Le Couche Tard. When she got there an hour later, Oliver was behind the bar with the bartender on duty — a dreadlocked Finnish woman —

and Georgia was drunk, on a stool, eating a bowl of popcorn. Oliver said he would make Kate her drink, a margarita, which, like the popcorn, was sweetened, rimmed with sugar rather than salt.

Techno music blared from the next room. Bodies moved together and came apart. Kate felt, as she did more often lately, that she was getting too old to be at a bar like this and doing a job like her job. In the euphoria of moving abroad and learning French and going to college, she'd neglected to think over the obvious question of what one did with a degree in art history. As her father had put it when she told her parents her major, "There aren't a lot of jobs for professional thinkers."

By the second margarita, she could feel herself sliding into a rut of self-pity. She told Georgia, who was encouraging Oliver to go dance with her when he was done mixing that TGV, that she was heading home.

"Cheers," Georgia said. "See you in the morning."

"Cheers," Oliver called, and Kate waved to him primly. That was the kind of man that Alexis had saved her from. She felt both grateful and lonely. She wanted to put her feet in Alexis's lap, and she told him so in the email she sent when she got home.

"I miss you, too," his response read the next morning. "I'm not jealous, but I don't like to think of you at a bar. Not saying you shouldn't go, of course. I hope the signs work. If not there is always the animal shelter. You can drop off Georgia while you're there."

Although Alexis and Georgia had spent little time in each other's presence — when he was in Grenoble, Kate mostly slept at his apartment — he had a strong opinion about her being exceedingly *vulgaire* and found her fascination with S&M distasteful.

"I can't get rid of her," Kate emailed back, "*mais ne t'inquiètes pas.* I'll get rid of the dog."

Later that day, the phone rang in the kitchen.

"Madame Kate Anderson?" a man said.

"Mademoiselle," she said.

"C'est la gendarmerie du centre-ville."

Kate, it seemed, had disobeyed *un arrêté* with her posters. One was not allowed to post *des affiches* without a permit.

"Désolée," she said. *"Je suis américaine."*

"Et alors," the man continued. Being American was no excuse for ignoring the law. There were clear procedures for lost animals. She should contact the proper

170

agency at the town hall, as well as the city's animal refuges to see if a listing had been made. If these attempts yielded nothing, she should bring the dog to the *fourrière communale,* where it would be kept for eight days before being sent to a refuge or, in the case of serious illness, euthanized. The posters, it went without saying, had been removed and Kate *était priée* to remove any others or she would be charged with a fine of three hundred francs.

A week went by. Alexis registered a patch of radiation in a forest in Finland. Kate opened the dishwasher and found a dildo in the top rack among the coffee bowls. An Ingres exhibit opened at the museum and she stayed late arranging pencil cases and coasters. The dog still hulked under the bench, head on its paws. She held on the phone for fifteen minutes with the town hall before hanging up.

"That's it," she told Georgia. "Off to the *fourrière communale.*"

It took both of them to coax the dog into Kate's Clio with the leash that Georgia provided. The dog trembled in the back seat, the seat belts clanking. To calm him down, Kate put on France Inter, which was playing "*le best de* Michael Jackson." The depot stood in Île Verte, halfway between downtown and the university, a suburb of sprawling concrete towers built during Grenoble's postwar, post-1968-Olympics boom. Most of the city looked this way. Just as the gift shop was a poor imitation of the museum, Grenoble, Kate often thought, was a poor imitation of Paris.

"He'll be euthanized, I'm afraid," the woman at the front desk said after she'd seen the dog. "We'll keep him for the eight days, but I can tell from here that he needs serious veterinary attention."

That night, six hundred francs of vet bills later, Kate returned home with the dog and walked him up to the house on his bandaged leg. She tugged at the leash. The dog didn't move. She unhooked the leash and he limped over to his usual place.

"I knew it," Georgia said when Kate came inside. "You couldn't." She was on the couch in a T-shirt, painting her toenails.

Kate explained what the vet had told her. The dog showed signs of malnutrition, fleas, tooth decay, conjunctivitis, and maggots, which had to be flushed out with alcohol from the hole in his leg. A hole made by teeth. "Something gnawed him," Kate said. "Rats probably."

Georgia dabbed at her pinkie toe. "You're

a sweetheart at heart," she said.

"She says we should keep him inside, but he doesn't want to come in."

"Watch the use of *we,* please," Georgia said. "I am only the kindly aunt."

"The pound was going to kill the dog," Kate wrote to Alexis that night. "I draw the line at murder."

Suddenly, then, the dog was her dog. After an initial email asking her if she could afford a pet, Alexis was supportive enough. Kate removed the dog's bandage and put on another, as instructed by the vet. She bought him a flea collar and a bag of enriched kibble. She started to prepare for Alexis's arrival, cleaned her bedroom and got a Brazilian wax. She was getting excited.

"You must be," Georgia said. "I don't know how you manage celibacy. I'd rather try cannibalism."

The dog refused to enter the house. When Kate, at the insistence of the vet during another visit, dragged him into the kitchen by his leash, he whined and pawed at the door. This would be a problem when temperatures dropped and the mountains around the city were capped with snow. For now, Kate was pleased by his preference. The dog might be her dog, at least for the moment, but she didn't enjoy him. He didn't cuddle or lick her feet or do the things dogs were supposed to do and that she wouldn't want anyway. She didn't like his gamey smell, and she didn't like bagging his shit. If anything, rather than falling in love with the dog, she felt a bit more in love with herself. She didn't know that she could be so generous. She thought of what her mother had said when her father broke his leg years before and Kate flew home to help. "This is the kind of endless sacrifice you save yourself from when you leave a marriage."

At the next visit, the vet said that with the dog's leg healed, Kate should start to take him for walks. She replaced Georgia's leash with a Starry Night leash from the gift shop, and one evening, a week before Alexis arrived, she and the dog headed along the path that climbed the hill of the Bastille. Once they'd come to the set of stairs that moved through tunnels and fortifications, the dog didn't hesitate. He tugged on the leash.

"You remember this place, don't you?" Kate said. *Tu t'en souviens.*" The dog pulled her through a fortification covered in graffiti and smelling of urine. They came to a viewpoint where the homeless encampment had been. Below, in the dusk, the tile rooftops of Grenoble glowed, as the rest of the city rolled toward the mountains. The *bulles* — translucent gondolas that carried visitors to the restaurant on top of the Bastille — hung motionless and empty over the river. From this height, the city was beautiful.

Kate undid the dog's leash. "Go on," she said. "Explore a little."

The dog limped into the trees. Kate stood by the opening of the tunnel. Used condoms, like jellyfish, lay on the ground. She could hear the dog burrowing in fallen leaves. It occurred to her that he might wander off. The Bastille was not a place for women to be alone at nightfall. She could be murdered, raped. Would Alexis be devastated? She called out for the dog. *"Chien?"* She walked off the trail, toward the sound of dry leaves. Under an oak tree, the dog was digging. She moved closer. The dog picked up something in his mouth and she saw that it was a dead bird, all bones and scraggly feathers. He dropped it at her feet.

A few months before he left for Sweden, Alexis had suggested that Kate meet his parents, Jacques and Hélène, who lived in a village now absorbed by the Parisian suburbs. The invitation came about after Kate said during dinner that Alexis might meet someone else when he was away in Stockholm. She herself would not, she said. "I'm not looking, and when I don't look I don't see."

"Je ne cherche pas non plus," he said.

"I think we have to discuss it." Her voice was calm, her face composed, but her heart skidded. She hated this feeling of vulnerability. They were having dinner at À Confesse, a *crêperie* decorated with pews and statues from a Catholic church. It seemed an appropriate place for the conversation. "Even people like us need a sign of commitment sometimes," she added. "You're leaving for a year."

"How about you come with me this weekend to meet my parents?" Alexis said. "My mother's been asking forever and my brother will be visiting with his family."

The drive to Benneville was the longest road trip that Kate had ever taken with a boyfriend, seven hours, not including a stop at a McDonald's in Clermont-Ferrand.

"Don't expect to see anything charming," Alexis said as they exited the *autoroute*. *"Benneville, c'est un trou."*

Kate saw what he meant as they drove over the Seine on an ugly chunk of a bridge,

176

then wound between roundabouts past *centres commerciaux* and warehouses. "There are a lot of car dealerships," she said.

"Because everyone wants to get out of here. We'll go somewhere more interesting next time."

Kate tried to spot the Seine between the gaps in the buildings. Next time, Alexis had said. They hadn't discussed the possibility of Kate visiting him in Stockholm. He hadn't asked, so she hadn't asked. This trip felt like a test. Everything was a test once you told someone that you loved them. Her nervousness grew as Alexis turned off the *nationale* onto a thinner road, into a forest. What if Alexis's parents didn't like her? What if she didn't like them? What if they really were as boring as Alexis had described, and in seeing him with them she found *him* boring? What if, like her boyfriend the first year of college, Alexis reverted with his parents, became annoyingly childish? She didn't want to fall out of love with Alexis, and as he pulled into the drive of a small house, Kate wanted to tell him to take her back home.

"*Voilà Maman,*" he said. A thin blond woman in breezy capris and a white blouse was walking out of the cottage.

"*Mon chou,*" she said to Alexis when he

and Kate got out of the car. She pinched Alexis's cheeks and kissed him on the forehead.

"*Arrête, Maman,*" he said. "She still thinks I'm ten," he added to Kate.

Hélène kissed Kate on the cheeks and said she was so glad to meet her. "You don't look like an American at all."

"What does an American look like?" Alexis asked.

"Bigger," Hélène said.

Alexis's father appeared from around the side of the cottage in a cardigan and rubber boots.

"We have heard much about you," he said to Kate in stilted English. Kate supposed this was an exaggeration. She didn't care. Already she was starting to relax. No one was paying too much attention to her. No one seemed to have expectations. The cottage, which had belonged to Alexis's grandparents, had been tastefully remodeled with light gray walls and white trim, and a stucco addition that housed a spacious kitchen. Hélène said that Kate and Alexis would sleep in the upstairs guestroom. "You'll be the first."

Alexis's brother, Emmanuel, drove up in a Deux Chevaux soon after, with his girlfriend, Cécile, and their four-year-old,

Adèle. Cécile looked as Kate had expected, a French *baba cool* wearing a sundress, with unshaven armpits. She was newly pregnant. The week before, Emmanuel had told his mother, who had told Alexis. "That's how things work in my family," Alexis had explained to Kate. "Like your American game of telephone. But they haven't told Adèle yet, so don't bring it up."

Cécile kissed Kate close to the mouth. She smelled like patchouli. "I always thought Alexis's girlfriends were pretend. Manu says you're American. The good kind or the bad kind?"

"I've lived in France for eight years," Kate said. "Doesn't that make me the good kind?"

"Belle et intelligente." Cécile winked at Alexis. She called to Adèle, who was plump, with a frizzy nest of hair. "Come meet your uncle's *grand amour.*"

Later, during the aperitif, Cécile talked about the women that she helped in the Paris suburbs, who came from Muslim countries. A mosque had been desecrated with graffiti, and she and her group were organizing a silent march and trying to keep the teenage boys of the *quartier* from burning cars at night in protest.

"The mayor is sure to send in the police,"

she said, lighting a cigarette. "This time next week, I'll probably be arrested."

"I'll break you out, *chérie,*" Emmanuel said, and blew her a kiss. He was scruffily handsome with a beard and ponytail, a chain-smoker like Cécile. He'd spent the previous week camped out on the site of a proposed hydrologic dam. As the adults talked, Adèle wandered around the lawn barefoot, building tepees out of pine needles and trying to whistle through blades of grass. She called her parents by their first names, because, Cécile explained to Kate, she and Emmanuel didn't believe in the traditional family hierarchy.

"Why should children automatically defer to their parents when so many parents are assholes?" she said.

"You got the one with the head on his shoulders," Hélène told Kate.

They were sitting near Jacques's vegetable garden, which fluffed and flopped over the fence. He'd gone to find forest mushrooms earlier with Adèle, and Hélène had baked the chanterelles into bite-size quiches. Kate had drunk two kir royals and the conversation came easy.

"Ready to go yet?" Alexis asked her later in bed, in the guestroom, under a skylight that showed the Big Dipper.

"I like them," Kate said.

"You can't tell that my mother and Cécile detest each other?"

"I picked up on a little tension."

For dinner Hélène had made vegetables from the garden — *poireaux à la crème,* and *lentilles* — with the roast. After taking a bite, Cécile asked what the lentils had been cooked in. When Hélène had said duck fat, Cécile spit the bite into her napkin and said she'd stick to baguette.

"Cécile thinks my mother is too bourgeois, and my mother thinks she's a flake and terrible for Manu."

"Mais elle semble m'aimer," Kate said.

Alexis rolled over and kissed her. "She likes you, but I wouldn't care if she didn't. I'm glad you're here."

After he fell asleep, Kate lay next to him, staring up at the Big Dipper, feeling as though she might cry. At some moment in all of her relationships, generally after a few months, she experienced the impossibility of being understood or of understanding the other person. She knew why she didn't want to get married or have children. Why didn't Alexis? If you were loved the way he was clearly loved by his parents and brother, you should want to repeat the experience. You should be like the couples in the museum courtyard with their dreamy eyes and big plans, their vows of eternal love exchanged in the shade of the Calder. It wasn't as if she wanted all that, but why didn't Alexis want it with her?

This feeling of alienation continued the next morning at breakfast as she ate one of the *pains au chocolat* that Hélène had picked up in town. Adèle was gone to play with a girl who lived up the drive in what everyone referred to as "the manor." Jacques came to the table with a basket of raspberries.

"Fresh from the fence," he said to Kate. "Try one. I don't use sprays."

"And to think how little he liked gardening once," Hélène said, laughing. "He's going to plant peas in the spring and lots of spinach. I'll make jars and jars of purée for the baby." She looked at Kate. "Alexis has told you the exciting news?"

"Let's not talk about it," Emmanuel said.

"Je ne peux pas résister," she said.

"Résiste, Maman," Emmanuel said sharply.

"We need to tell you something," Cécile said. She was smoking a pipe, and looked more annoyed than upset.

"I think I'll go take a walk in the forest," Kate said.

"You can stay," Alexis said.

"*Ça va,*" she said. "I'll give you all privacy."

She hurried toward the drive that ran by the cottage, not wanting to hear any of the conversation. She could see the manor in the distance. On a spill of overgrown grass, Adèle sat with a girl of twelve or so who, after Kate said hello, introduced herself as Élodie.

"*Elle est américaine comme toi,*" Adèle said.

"Really?" Kate asked.

"Yes," Élodie said, in perfect English. "I live in Syracuse. We spend the summers here, though."

She was a pretty girl, tiny, as if she would float away on a gust of wind. She and Adèle were weaving dandelion chains.

"You live in that big house?" Kate said.

Élodie nodded.

"Lucky."

Élodie shrugged. "It's a little boring here. There aren't any kids. I like when Adèle visits. This might be our last summer, though. We have to rent it out. It costs too much to keep up."

Kate said goodbye. She never quite knew how to talk to children. She wondered what Cécile had announced about the baby. A miscarriage, maybe. Or maybe she and Emmanuel were moving away from Paris with Adèle. Hélène would have to ship her homemade baby food via *La Poste.* That kind of news, she was sure, would devastate Hélène. Kate's mother, on the other hand, had only been to visit twice from Florida since Kate moved to Grenoble. Her father had met her in Paris with her stepmother several times on their way to other parts of Europe. He didn't like the French. He found them snotty. "I don't understand how you ended up here," he said, as Kate asked the waiter for ketchup for his *pommes frites,* and requested that the chef put the sauce *à la crème* on the side for her stepmother. Alexis would not like her parents. And when would he meet them? Maybe never? She picked up her pace until her heart went faster. Exercise always made her feel better, and by the time she returned to the drive a half hour later, she had relaxed. The girls were gone from the grass. Behind the cottage, Hélène and Jacques sat alone at the table.

"I'm sorry, dear," Hélène said to Kate. "We are a bit overcome. I'm afraid that Cécile lost the baby."

"Je suis désolée," Kate stammered.

Jacques rubbed Hélène's arm. "Life is very complicated."

"Emmanuel and Cécile had to head back home." Hélène's smile was strained. "They said to tell you goodbye. Alexis is out front packing the car. We'll walk you out." She stood up. "It's been such a pleasure, dear."

"I thought we were leaving after lunch," Kate said as she and Alexis drove away from the cottage. Alexis had barely looked at his parents when he kissed them goodbye.

"I wanted to get out of there fast."

"Your mother told me about the baby. I'm sorry."

"She told you that Cécile miscarried, didn't she?"

"Yes."

"That's not what happened." He pulled onto the main road. "Cécile had an abortion two days ago. The pregnancy was an accident. Emmanuel wasn't supposed to tell us until she decided what she wanted to do." They were driving along the Seine now, past factories and apartment towers. "You missed World War Three. My mother cried. My father looked like he was going to have a stroke. Then after Manu and Cécile left, my mother said I should tell you it was a miscarriage. I said I wouldn't. She got upset again, and I went inside to pack."

"Maybe she was trying to protect me," Kate said.

"*Non.* She was making things seem nicer than they are. That's what she does. And

185

my father lets her."

As they drove out of Benneville, Alexis talked, more than he'd ever talked to her at one time. He told her about his uncle, Guy, a schizophrenic whom he'd only mentioned before in passing. "He's been in and out of institutions all his life. Once, when I was eleven and he'd just been released again, my parents let him stay with us for a night. My mother put a mattress on the floor of the room Emmanuel and I shared. After everyone was asleep, Guy woke me up and told me to come with him to the bathroom. He made me sit on the toilet and said not to move. He kneeled down in front of me and rolled up his sleeve. He took a razor out of his shirt pocket. I started to cry. I thought he was going to kill me. He told me to be quiet, 'quiet as a lamb,' he said. Then he cut the skin of his arm from the wrist to the elbow. He did it again. And again. I was so scared, I wet myself. He made five cuts, deep enough that his arm bled. Then he kissed me on the forehead and told me to go back to bed. I didn't change out of my pajamas. I was awake all night, waiting for the bedroom door to open. But he didn't come back. He slept on the couch. The next morning, I told my mother I'd wet the bed and gave her the pajamas. Guy was in the kitchen, having breakfast with my father. It was as if it hadn't happened."

"And you never said anything to your parents?"

"No, but they should have figured it out. I was a mess after that for months. I kept waking up with nightmares. Anyway, who lets someone that screwed up stay alone with their kid?" Alexis looked over at her. "This is the first time I've told anyone about it."

"I'll never repeat it," Kate said, taking his hand.

And that had been the sign that she'd needed.

Alexis arrived at the Lyon airport a week later.

"We're so glad to see each other," he said after they kissed in the terminal and again in the parking lot. *"On est ridicule."*

"We love each other," Kate said. "That's why we're ridiculous."

"Ce chien est super triste," he said when they got to the house. That is one sad dog.

"I told you," Kate said.

They spent the next two hours in bed, making love, and then both fell asleep.

When Kate woke up, the windows were

dark. She went downstairs to the bathroom. Georgia sat on the edge of the tub, crying.

"I'm sorry," she said. "I was trying not to make any noise." She and Oliver, she explained, had a fight.

"He's been shagging that bartender at Le Couche Tard. He said he thought we had an open relationship."

Kate smelled that acidic tang in the air. She sat down next to Georgia and put her arm around her shoulders.

"I thought you didn't believe in monogamy."

"I don't, but that's different from saying we had an open relationship." Georgia started to cry again. "Bollocks. I'm sorry. Drama queen. I can leave. Your first night with Monsieur Havre."

"Stay," Kate said. "We were going to order a pizza."

"It's okay," Alexis said when she told him that Georgia was home. "I'm glad we're spending our first night with your smelly dog and your fucked-up roommate. That's how much I've missed you."

She laughed. "Try to be nice, please."

He did try. Downstairs, he said hello to Georgia and pretended not to notice her runny nose and smudged eyeliner. He opened a bottle of wine. Kate put on David

Bowie. The pizza arrived on the back of a moped. Georgia picked off the *lardons* and ate them first, then the cheese, then the crust, as she asked Alexis polite, unflirty questions about his research. Kate moved her foot against Alexis's under the table and he pressed back.

They'd just finished eating when someone knocked on the front door. Georgia went to the window. "It's Oliver," she said. "He'll go away." She opened the freezer and took out a container of ice cream. "So kind of like what you use to find old coins in the ground?" she asked Alexis, who had been explaining radiation detectors. The knocking slowed.

"Fucking hell," Oliver shouted. There was a yelp.

"That's the dog." Kate ran to the door.

Outside, the dog was under the bench, and Oliver was holding his leg.

"What happened?" she said.

"Fucker bit me." Oliver looked past her, at Georgia. "I'm so sorry, chicken," he said. "You're the only good thing in my life and now I've messed that up too."

"I'll get some Betadine," Georgia said.

Kate kneeled next to the bench to see the dog.

"*Tu saignes?*" Alexis asked Oliver.

189

Oliver rolled up his pant leg. "Right. You're a doctor."

"Not that kind of doctor," Alexis said.

The dog was trembling. "Did you kick him?" Kate asked.

"I had to get him off me. Could that thing have rabies?"

"He's up to date with his shots." Kate put her hand on the dog's back.

"You might need stitches," Georgia said. She'd come back outside with the bottle of Betadine. "I'll take you to the hospital. You're too drunk to drive yourself."

"Georgy," Oliver said. "Baby."

"Shut up and let me pour some of this on your leg," she said.

"Jesus," Alexis said after they'd gone. "They are a nightmare."

"I'm worried he broke one of the dog's ribs," Kate said.

As they did the dishes together, Kate kept thinking about the dog. He hadn't wanted to come inside, so she'd put a blanket over him. When she went outside to check how he was, he'd stopped shaking. "That guy is an ass," she said, petting his head. "I'm glad you bit him."

Back from the hospital, Georgia got a bottle of Chartreuse and three glasses from the cupboard, and they all sat on the couch.

"I dropped Oliver off at the entrance to the *urgences,*" she said, after downing her drink. "I wasn't going to sit around waiting. I told him to call here when he was done."

"You're picking him up?" Alexis said.

Georgia poured herself another Chartreuse. "He does seem sorry. Maybe the whole open relationship thing really was a misunderstanding."

"He's manipulating you," Alexis said. "You can't trust a guy like that."

"A guy like that?" Georgia laughed. "Sorry, Alexis. You're just a different kind of 'guy like that.' This is the first time you've even spent the night here."

"He can't get off without tying you up."

"Don't talk about things you don't understand."

"Please don't fight," Kate said, her voice straining. She felt as if she were outside with the dog, watching the two of them through the window. Alexis's face softened. "Sorry," he said to Georgia. "My uncle did something fucked up to me when I was a kid. So I don't like domination games."

"Who didn't have someone do something fucked up to them as a kid?" Georgia said. "Me, it was my mom's handyman. Had me sit on his lap and told me to wiggle."

"It wasn't like that," Alexis said. And then,

before Kate could stop him, he was telling Georgia about the night in his parents' apartment, with the same details he'd mentioned that day in his car, matter-of-factly, as if he'd said the words a thousand times.

"Why did you tell her about Guy?" Kate asked him after Georgia had gone to bed.

"I don't know," Alexis said. "Maybe talking to you about it opened me up. Maybe I'm changing."

She got the leash from next to the door. "I should walk the dog."

"I don't understand why you're angry."

"Try to figure it out while I'm gone."

The dog came out from under the blanket. She started to put on his leash, and instead left it on the bench. They walked out of the yard, up the street, to the Bastille. The night was hazy with smog. The dog stayed next to her on the path, and on the stairs fell a tread behind. Below, the boulevards of Grenoble flashed with veins of lights that ran out of the city and became the sprinkled lights of the pavilions, then the dark rise of the mountains. Kate waited as the dog urinated on a tree. Would Alexis understand why she was angry? If he didn't, she couldn't see staying with him. She joined the dog on the steps. They passed the rampart where, a few weeks before, she'd slowed her pace to fling the dead bird over the edge. She could picture what the skeleton had looked like as it fell, a ghost made of bones, winging over the city.

THE POND

1910

The snow arrived in Benneville during the
night, changing the meanest roof and horse
cart into sparkling, magical objects. On the
hill behind the school, the boys were using
their satchels for sleds as the girls sculpted
snowmen and castles. The postman plowed
his bicycle down two streets of his route
before giving up and going to the café,
where the *patron* served hot chocolate on
the house. *Quelle merveille,* people said as
they shoveled the sidewalks and streets.
Quelle surprise. But for Émile Vouette, who
was following his sons out the door of
his manor, the snow hadn't been made new
by the years spent away from his native
village, which bridged a river in the Vosges
Mountains. The boys' exclamations, the
astonishment on their faces, were reminders
of what he couldn't tell them. This snowfall
was nothing compared to the snow he'd

once known.

Charles and François ignored the path the driver had made to the carriage and instead waded, calf-deep, through the drifts.

"Can you believe it, *monsieur*?" Charles called to the driver, who shook his head. *"C'est un miracle."*

"We can build a fort." François tossed a handful of snow into the air. "Or even a fortress."

"It must be trillions of flakes," Charles said, "and every one is different."

"Venez." Émile climbed into the *barouche.* "You will be soaked."

He laid the fur rug over his knees, giving the other edge to the boys once they'd sat down. The driver clucked at the horses, and the wheels creaked down the drive, past the crystalized forest. As Charles told François about snowflakes, Émile thought the words he couldn't say. It isn't as I've told you. I wasn't born in Paris. I was born on the other side of the country, where this miracle took place all the time, where my sisters and I skied to school with coals in our pockets, wishing that what our grandmother said was true: The snow was the molting feathers of the storks that had abandoned their nests until the next spring.

In the parlor of the manor, Émile's wife, Geneviève, sat down at the piano. She set a battered copy of *Leçons pour débutant* on the music rack and clipped her pince-nez on her nose. With the doors shut, the walls of the room closed around her like a silk glove. A fire crackled calmly in the chimney. Upstairs, the maids were making the beds and emptying the chamber pots. In the kitchen, the cook was rolling out a *pâte brisée* for the almond *tarte* that Geneviève had requested for lunch. The household, Geneviève knew, would run very well without her. All she needed to do was to point and to make lists.

She opened the book to the C-major scale. When she'd woken up in her room and the housekeeper told her as she opened the shutters, "*Regardez, madame.* Everything is white," Geneviève had worried that the boys and Émile would be unable to leave. The carriage, though, was long gone down the drive, and her body was loose with guilty relief. Straightening her back, she rested her fingers on the keys, two octaves down from middle C. She locked her gaze on the black notes and began. Her hands felt unwieldy.

The hesitant notes didn't match the sure notes in her head.

The piano, though old, was in perfect tune. Since her marriage to Émile, it had stood here by the window, as it once stood in the home Geneviève shared with her father, dusted and waxed by the servants, tuned every year, not to be touched, a monument to Geneviève's mother, who had died in childbirth. A few months ago, Geneviève had opened the seat, as she'd done often before, to look through her mother's scribbles on the pages of the primers and sheet music: notes about resting, circled sharps, the doodle of an exasperated face. This time, she sat down. Since, she'd come to the piano every morning once the boys and Émile had left for Benneville, the doors shut on the servants. She'd told the housekeeper that she'd rather Monsieur not know. Why trouble him with her silly pastime when he had so much on his mind? She hit the A major instead of the C major. She started again.

Charles watched from the front of the classroom as the *maître d'école* lowered the map to trace the path of the winds that had met over their heads.

"What you find astonishing," the schoolmaster said, "science does not."

From the north, east, and west, ocean mixed with glaciers, Normandy with the Vosges and the Vendée, but more than this, Charles thought as the pointer moved across the map, the igloos of Eskimos, the volcanoes of the Azores. The snow was a promise made to him by the world beyond the world he knew. You fell asleep in your same bed to the same sound of your brother's breathing, under the same window with the same view of the forest and gardens, and during the night, behind the shutters, everything changed. Even his father, when he kissed their cheeks in front of the school before heading to the mill, seemed another father, with lively cheeks and glistening eyes. And François had listened at full attention as Charles explained the perfect geometry of snowflakes, which he'd read about that morning in his encyclopedia. Each flake, he told François, was the same hexagonal prism built around a dust mote that swept up water vapor as it fell, sprouting feathered arms. Now, a row of desks away, François stared away from the map and out the window, thinking, Charles knew, of the weight of the rifle against his shoulder, the way the sky would shrink to one small arrow.

"The snow is a sign," he'd said to Charles as they walked into the schoolroom. "Today we go out."

By late morning, the men out felling trees in the forest had given up and returned to the mill, and the logs on the Seine barely moved through the scabs of ice. In the yard, the men slipped as they yanked on the leads of the plow horses, and inside, the sawdust on the floor had become a layer of mud. Émile looked down from the observation deck, waiting for a log to whir through the saw. For the past hour, from his office window, he'd watched the snow start up again, though lightly. Now he rang the closing bell.

"Go home to your families," he called down to the men. "I've seen children crossing the bridge. The master must have let them out early."

The men looked up at him, surprised. A few years before, when one of them had caught his sleeve in the saw, Émile ran down the stairs and, having sent for the doctor, hid the man's severed hand in his coat pocket. For a while after, the men had lost some of their reserve with Émile, but now, again, they stood back as he passed by and murmured their thanks into their collars.

199

Outside, he clenched his ankles to root his steps to the sidewalk. Snowflakes peppered the air, caught in his beard. A cluster of women, cocooned in shawls, were talking on a corner.

"It must be half a meter," one of them said, and then, "*Bonjour, bonjour,* Monsieur Vouette," as Émile walked by.

He tipped his hat, moving faster, off the sidewalk and into the road and the paths left by carriage wheels. The stone façades of the village glowed in the fresh light. Icicles dangled from the roof of the train station. Ice cataracted the ditches that bordered the road. When Émile was a boy, frozen puddles had meant that the river would freeze soon, and that he and his sisters could put on their skates. First, though, they had to wait on the shore for their father to measure the depth of the ice with his chisel, point out the shadowy patches to avoid, and remind them what to do if they heard cracking: Don't panic. Keep skating, and the ice won't know your true weight.

Geneviève had the C-major scale now, or rather her hands did. The trick had been to look away from the notes. The movement of snow out the window had distracted her eyes from the page, releasing her fingers, which moved faster, left hand joining her right, spiders creeping at first, now more like sparrows flying. The window sashes fused with the glass. Beyond, the trees fused with the sky. The snowflakes turned and fell and twisted. Her fingers lifted, rested, pressed, and paused. The notes poured into the room, drowning the glossy furniture and rich carpets with a better beauty. Her hands had their own brain, their own memory. They had nothing to do with her. And they knew exactly what they were doing.

In the old servants' cottage, Charles waited as François disappeared into the fireplace, a crude hole cut into the stone wall. The first time François had done this, two weeks before, he'd wanted to see if he could get to the roof. Now, as then, his boots reappeared and he ducked back into the room with the Chassepot rifle, the weapon, Charles had learned from his encyclopedia, that had been issued to soldiers during the Franco-Prussian War. He and François had decided that it must have belonged to a servant of Monsieur Léger who had deserted that distant front.

They walked out the back door of the cottage, past a room filled with coal. The muzzle of the rifle poked from under François's coat. Over the past week, they'd cleaned the rust from the chamber and improvised a papier-mâché sabot from their father's newspaper and the maid's ironing starch. François got a lead bullet and a bag of gunpowder from one of his friends, who, unlike him, spent their weekends hunting in the forest. When they were smaller, their father said he didn't believe in hunting, that he found it prehistoric. Wild animals aren't healthy, he'd say. Better to eat the chickens and pigs that the cook bought at market. When François turned ten and asked for a rifle to shoot pinecones, their father said that he didn't believe in boys carrying guns. *"Il invente des raisons,"* François told Charles. He's making up reasons. "He must be a pacifist," Charles said, and then he'd explained the term.

Sometimes, when he fell asleep, Émile remembered the childhood in Paris that he'd invented for himself as if it were real. He saw the sickly mother in the small bed in the dingy corner in place of his own mother, who had been quick and loud. He smelled sewers rather than pine, heard the accent of the Alsatian grandmother who gave him his slight accent. The sisters he saw best because they had the same round

202

cheeks and blond hair as his own sisters, but they played on streets rather than in the forest. His father still drank Schnapps; in sidewalk cafés, not in his armchair by the fire.

The first time that he and Geneviève had walked together to the pond — the mill foreman and the mill owner's daughter — she went first with her story. She told him about the heaviness of her father's grief. "He has never reproached me," she said. "Still, how could he not? I took away the person he most loved." Her hand was tucked in Émile's elbow, and he felt his heart pulse as they stood by the water. She told him about a memory she had of her mother smiling down at her through masses of curly hair. "It makes no sense," she said. "She died only hours after I was born. I know it sounds silly. But you understand, don't you? My father told me you lost both of your parents."

It was in that moment that Émile had been a true coward. He shouldn't have nodded sadly. He shouldn't have pretended to share her grief. He should have told her the truth about himself. He should have trusted her, as she trusted him. If he had, maybe right now he wouldn't be looking at the side of her face, but into her eyes again. He'd come back into the dining room from washing his hands to find her alone at the long table, the coffeepot steaming, the boys gone.

"I told them to go enjoy the snow," she said.

Geneviève drank her coffee quickly, not bothering with sugar, willing Émile to do the same, to go back to the mill. If she practiced her scales for another week, she might try her first song. When she'd seen the boys come down the drive, early from school, she'd been looking at the sheet music for "Alouette." Her mother had drawn a star next to the title. Geneviève knew the tune from the boys' old music box. As she read the notes on the staff, she could hear them start to play. On her lap, her fingers moved. Then the boys had appeared and the music stopped. She'd taken off her pince-nez, put the primer and sheet music back into the seat, opened the parlor door, called to the housekeeper, became *madame* again, a mother again. She met the boys at the stairs, under the chandelier. They should take off their boots and warm their feet by the fire in the parlor, she told them. The housekeeper was getting them tisanes and blankets. And for lunch, the cook was making their favorite dessert.

■ ■ ■ ■

Charles sat next to François on a heap of stones near the frozen pond. The bare willow tree branches were anchored in ice. The clouds had gone, taking the snow.

"They won't be long," François said, watching the sky. "They come by all the time."

"We'll hear them before we see them," Charles said.

It was wasteful what they were doing — hunting for the sake of hunting. But it would be worth it. As winter became spring, there would be more secret excursions into the forest, more bullets, more talking low from their beds at night, more of this togetherness. Rabbits and boar. A deer, maybe.

"*Ils arrivent,*" François said as the honking began. He raised the rifle.

"Poachers," Geneviève said when Émile went to the window.

"No," he said. "Not this late in the season."

He knew that sound like the sound of his own breathing. Not the high shirr of a hunting rifle; the sharp pop of bullet meant to rip apart flesh and shatter bone.

"Où vas-tu," Charles said as François laid down the rifle and stepped onto the ice. In the middle of the pond, the goose had stopped thumping its wings. The honking from above had faded. The flock moved back into its V, a gap at the end. "We said we'd leave it."

François took another step. "We'll give it to the cook. Mother will be happy not to have to plan dinner."

"But then Father will know we went hunting," Charles said, and then he realized that this had been François's plan all along. "He won't change his mind."

"Yes he will. You'll see. He'll have to let me shoot then."

"You should have told me," Charles said. "I wouldn't have come."

"Rentre, alors." François slid toward the goose.

Charles picked up the rifle and walked toward the trees. As he reached the trail, François called out his name.

Out the back doors of the manor, through the blank sheet of the garden, Émile walked quickly, although the bolt of terror that ripped through his stomach at the sound of the shot had calmed to worry. He followed the trail of the boys' footprints toward the forest gate. On the battlefield, there'd been no clear way between the corpses. That other boy's face, the mirror image of Émile's face, had appeared out of nowhere, loose with surprise, then with fear, then gone — a charred hole where there had been eyes, nose, mouth. Émile had run for the trees, the Chassepot banging against his leg, but he didn't let go, keeping it with him in the barn where he hid that night and then in the traveling trunk a farmer gave him, along with a set of clothes. The rifle stayed with him, at the bottom of the trunk, as he traveled farther, working on barges that brought him to the Seine, and on to a job at the mill, leaving behind the boy he had been and the soldier that boy had become until he was, these years and kilometers later, a man without a coat, stumbling through the snow, looking for his sons.

"It's breaking up," François called. Charles could see the web of cracks under his brother's feet, could feel the bite of the water. He held his breath and didn't blink. It seemed that one movement, one flutter in the universe, might be enough to make François go under.

207

■ ■ ■ ■

The trail turned toward the pond, and
Émile saw Charles, the rifle in his arms. A
tube of metal and a handle of wood. A
thing, like a log or a pair of skis. And
ridiculous even, the way Charles balanced it
between his elbows, as Émile himself had
done in the woods behind his house, the
first time he hunted boar with his father,
before he learned how to drop in the bullet
and fill the chamber with powder, before he
learned how to kill.

Charles heard his father's voice before he
saw him. "Son." His face was full of what
could only be called joy that disappeared
when he broke from the forest and had a
full view of the pond. "Move," he shouted
to François. "I can't," François called. Or
did he? When he thought back on this moment, Charles would only hear one thing
clearly: "I'll come get you. But you have to
come toward me. You have to keep skating."

As evening fell, Geneviève stood on the
balcony, wrapped in a shawl, watching the
men break open the pond. Under their picks
and axes, the white ice collapsed into the

black water. They'd uncovered enough to slip in a fishing skiff. "You will remember something else about your father," she'd told the boys as she held them in the snowy garden. "You don't know what yet. But something else." After she'd put them to bed and closed their shutters, she sent the servants home. She locked the parlor door from the hallway and dropped the key down the kitchen drain. Now, she took her hands from under the shawl and held them on the cold metal until they burned.

Charles saw the men return from the forest through the shutters he'd opened at the sound of scraping snow. They pulled a fishing skiff, and inside was his father. After he and François had looked in the hole in the ice, before they ran back to the manor, François took the rifle from Charles and dropped it into the pond. Only years later did Charles understand why François got rid of the rifle, when he was at university in Lyon and one night, as he walked along the Saône, the puzzle came together. "You knew, didn't you," he asked François when he next saw him, "that Papa was the deserter?" They were sitting in a café across from the Gare du Nord, waiting to ship out to the front. But François only shrugged and lit another cigarette. "*Maman* was right," he said. "I don't remember much of anything from back then. It's like it happened to someone else."

Two years later, in the trenches of Verdun, Charles crawled under the barbwire, through the sulfurous mud, to one of his men, who was screaming for help. He hooked his arm around the man's neck and dragged him back to the trench under fire from the Germans. His men spoke of this moment years later, to their wives and mistresses and sons, to fellow veterans on the Fête de l'Armistice. They described the terror in Charles's face as he clawed his way toward the sky. They tried to explain how they felt when the wounded man dropped into the trench several eternal minutes later, followed by Charles. Many of them said that they'd survived the war because of this rescue, because of the hope it gave them, because of this proof of what some called the human spirit and others called courage. The Croix de Guerre that Charles received hung in the thin hallway of his apartment in Strasbourg, and the few people who visited thought that this quiet academic had a streak of bravado and arrogance, unaware that the medal had little to do with that night in the trenches and everything to do with an afternoon when Charles stood on the shore of a frozen pond and watched his father rush toward his brother. And although François, killed in the Second Battle of the Marne four months before the armistice, never learned about his brother's act, Charles knew that if he had survived he would have understood.

TINTIN IN THE ANTILLES

2006

"This," Adèle said. She presented the coconut to Hélène like a decapitated head. They were standing in the exotic fruits section of the *hypermarché,* next to clusters of bananas and a pyre of mandarins. Hélène had said that her granddaughter must choose a fruit for dessert tonight, since she'd had an ice cream already. She thought Adèle would pick bananas that she could flambé with rum, or pears that she might poach and serve on a raft of *crème anglaise.*

"I've never cooked a coconut," she said.

"You told me I could choose anything."

Though ten, Adèle had the boxy neck and drop to her chin of a middle-aged woman. Her body, dressed in black leggings and a black sweater and black leather flats, was as compact and formless as a button mushroom stump.

"Bon, alors." Hélène took the coconut to

the weighing station. "You'll have to hold it tight or it will roll to the floor and then I'll have to pay for the crack in the tile."

As Adèle anchored the coconut on the scale, Hélène tried to find the picture on the computer screen, tapping past nectarines and turnips. A line formed behind, and she heard the restrained sighs, the shuffle of feet, the irritated patience that passed as kindness now that she was old. She touched the back arrow. The screen jumped to potatoes and yams and onions — red, green, sweet, pickling, Spanish, shallots; how could the world contain so many onions?

"Perhaps it's with the bananas," she said to Adèle.

"My arms are getting tired," Adèle replied. Now she was in the lettuces. Mâche. Endive. Frisée. She pressed the arrow. This was how Jacques felt all the time. Earlier, in the cottage, before the nurse arrived, Hélène had turned her back for only a moment to pin up her hair in the armoire mirror, and he'd disappeared. She found him downstairs in the coat closet. Pajama bottoms around his ankles, he was urinating into a rubber boot. She touched the arrow again.

"I believe they are sold by the piece, *madame*," a man's voice said from behind.

213

"You will find nothing there."

"We never see these," the cashier said when Hélène gave him the coconut. It cost seven euros.

"A fortune." Hélène sighed as she handed the bag to Adèle. "But the little one wants to try it."

Adèle's visit, only four hours in, had soured the moment she arrived in the back seat of her father's Citroën. First, Hélène had slipped up and, after hugging Adèle in front of the cottage, said, *"Mais qu'elle est grosse!"* instead of *"Mais qu'elle est grande!"* and Emmanuel had said to Adèle, "Don't listen to your grandmother. Your uncle and I never did."

Adèle smiled back at him, that same sharp, quick smile that sliced into her cheeks like a knife in pastry dough.

"Have you had her thyroid checked?" Hélène asked Emmanuel as Adèle brought her bag upstairs to the guestroom. "You know what your brother says about us all having been irradiated by the Russians."

"It isn't her thyroid." Emmanuel lit a cigarette. "It's pastries. Don't talk to her about it. That's how you mess girls up."

Hélène had said nothing and brought him an ashtray, but how could a child balloon like that in only a year? The last time Hélène and Jacques visited Emmanuel and his family in Paris, Adèle had only one chin.

Then Emmanuel couldn't stay for the coffee and the palmiers that Hélène had baked especially for him. He wanted to get back to the city before the noon traffic clogged the *périphérique.* He didn't even go upstairs to see Jacques, even though Hélène told him that his father was in the bedroom with the nurse.

"He doesn't know who I am anyway," he said.

He kissed Hélène on the cheeks, kissed Adèle, lit another cigarette, and said he'd be back in two days.

"You have a baby," Hélène told Adèle as the Citroën disappeared down the road, "and you love him more than anything. And then one day, he won't stay for coffee."

"Do you have an Internet signal?" Adèle had taken out her phone.

"No," Hélène said, too sharply, "but we have frogs in the well."

After the problem of the Internet signal, there had been the problem of the duck. When Hélène brought Adèle to the kitchen so she could see what was making that delicious smell, Adèle informed her that like her mother, Cécile, she didn't eat meat.

"Duck isn't meat. It's poultry," Hélène said.

"I don't eat anything with feet, eyes, or feathers."

"Well, then" — Hélène closed the door to the oven — "we shall go to the store and find you something that you can eat."

First, though, as planned, she took Adèle to the Benneville square, which had been decorated with flying bells and eggs for Easter, and then to the *glacerie* for an ice cream. Unfortunately, the *glacerie* had a signal.

"Pas à table," she'd told Adèle, who put away her phone begrudgingly. Hélène tried to make conversation (Did Adèle like school? Was she still taking oboe lessons?) as Adèle ate her Dame Blanche with abandon, the spoon whipping to her lips and back into the glass tulip of ice cream. Done, Adèle dashed the napkin over her mouth and asked if now she could use her phone. She'd left off in the middle of some kind of game and had robots to kill.

"Ten minutes," Hélène said, as she used to tell Emmanuel and Alexis when they wanted to run in the forest before dinner on a visit to their grandparents, back when they owned the cottage. Adèle's thumbs flew. Hélène signaled for the check. It was then that she had started to feel indignant, even mean. Across the table, Adèle had inflated from a plump girl to a fat girl, from quiet to sullen, from slightly tiring to exhausting. And Adèle, she thought now, must have sensed the hardening. This was why, when, on the way out of Benneville, they stopped at the *hypermarché* to choose something Adèle could eat for dinner and Hélène told her that she must choose a fruit as a base for the dessert that would follow a cheese pizza seemingly big enough for a family of eight, Adèle had picked the most difficult fruit imaginable.

"You know" — Hélène navigated the car through the sprawling parking lot of the *hypermarché* — "we didn't even have a television when your father was growing up. Can you imagine?"

"No." In the rearview mirror, Adèle was a fatter, smaller version of Cécile. "I'll have two televisions now."

"Will you?"

"And two bedrooms. The one at Cécile's opens onto the roof. She says we can go out there sometimes to have tea." Adèle scrunched deeper in her seat. *"On peut voir l'Arc de Triomphe."*

"Can you?" Hélène turned the car onto the main road. "How lovely. Is the roof flat?"

"I don't know. I haven't seen the apartment yet. Emmanuel is going to take me there tomorrow."

"I hope the roof is indeed flat, or that could be dangerous."

Adèle didn't answer. Really, Hélène thought, how could Cécile fill the child's head with such nougat? "Cécile and I need more space," Emmanuel had told Hélène when he called to ask if Adèle could stay during the move. "Adèle isn't upset about it, but it would be better not to have her underfoot." He announced what anyone else would call a separation with the same blasé tone that he'd announced on the phone a decade ago that Cécile was pregnant and that they were moving in together: "No, *Maman,* not getting married. We don't believe in all that."

This was not long after he'd called to say that he'd dropped out of university to backpack across the Orient. He and Cécile met in a souk in Istanbul and returned to Paris together to work with the immigrants in the suburbs, where men beat their wives and women wore headscarves even in summer. Hélène was not "anti-immigrant," as Emmanuel had accused her of once — she was quite attached to the Portuguese woman who cleaned the cottage, and Jacques's nurse was from Poland or Hungary, one of those Eastern European countries. Still, she did think that if you were going to move to France you should want to be French. Alexis's wife, Kate, for instance, might be American, but she didn't throw it in Hélène's face. She appreciated Hélène's cooking and asked her opinion about how to decorate the house they'd recently bought near Grenoble. Together, they'd found a pretty yellow for what would be the nursery.

Unlike Kate, Cécile never wore makeup, had a ring in her nose, and smoked a pipe after breakfast. Once he'd met her, Emmanuel's leftward leanings had fallen fully west, as Jacques put it in his gentle, detached way. Emmanuel listened to American jazz. He voted for the Green Party, and had been arrested for pulling up GMO corn near Arles. He thought marijuana should be legal. He and Cécile didn't go to church ever, not even at Christmas. And Cécile liked to hurt Hélène, as if Hélène represented everything about her own generation that Cécile's generation wanted to destroy. They'd had a terrible blowout some years back, after Cécile had an abortion and mentioned it as casually as if the baby were one of the warts the doctor froze off Hélène's toes.

Hélène had been horrified. She had looked

to Jacques to step in, and he didn't. He never took sides in these situations. It had been one of the worst days of Hélène's life, until the one when Jacques had his stroke. She'd sobbed herself to sleep for weeks, sudden surges of weeping that left her spent. It wasn't only the thought of that baby's soul; it was the cruelty that Cécile had displayed and thus that Emmanuel had displayed. Finally, a year later, when the ice had melted, she asked him why they had told her about the baby in the first place. He said that he was sorry. "I didn't know that's what we would end up deciding," he said. "I thought we would have it."

She'd felt so sorry for him then that she'd forgiven him, but she would never forgive Cécile. Emmanuel hadn't meant to be cruel to her. He'd told her about the pregnancy because he'd wanted the baby. And Cécile had punished him for telling Hélène by announcing the abortion so casually. Or maybe — Hélène thought in very dark moments — Cécile had punished him for telling Hélène by having the abortion at all. Hélène would always connect the death of that baby to Jacques's stroke, even though Alexis, when she'd said this to him, said there was no one to blame and then calmly explained artery blockages.

When she and Adèle walked back into the cottage, Jacques was moaning. Adèle stopped by the door.

"It's all right," Hélène said, "your grand-father makes noises sometimes."

"It sounds like a ghost."

"It isn't. Let's take this to the kitchen."

It did sound like a ghost, she thought, as Adèle, still big-eyed, followed her down the hall with the bag of groceries. The moaning started with a rattle inside Jacques's throat and then bloomed out of his mouth. You couldn't stop it, though she knew that the nurse was trying, running her hand down Jacques's arm, telling him, *Tout va bien, tout va bien,* plumping the pillows behind his head.

She told Adèle to take the pizza to the deep freezer in the storage room down the hall. She stepped into the kitchen, which had been added on to the house years before. At the time, she had delighted in moving over the threshold from the old house into this modern room with its fresh tile floors and straight walls, and all the counter space in the world. Now, though, the addition felt like a mistake, like a taut, lifted face on an old neck that only made the neck look older.

She unwrapped the coconut from its

plastic-bag shroud. The kitchen smelled of the cold duck. She emptied the fruit bowl, blown from cobalt glass and fluted at the top. Jacques had given it to her on their twenty-fifth wedding anniversary, one of his many practical gifts. She put the coconut in the bowl and arranged the plums and oranges around it. The moaning faded, and then started again. Why did the ocean look blue, she wondered, when it was transparent? She had learned this in school, surely. The Atlantic was gray in Brittany and blue in the south. The skies of Brittany were gray and the skies in the south blue. So the water must reflect the color of the sky.

"There." She put the fruit bowl on the table. "Doesn't that look nice?"

Adèle clumped into a chair. "He does that all the time?"

"Why don't you get the peg solitaire from the parlor?" Hélène said. "We'll play a game here. I'll go check on your grandfather first."

Upstairs, in the bedroom, Jacques sat by the gabled window, staring out at the forest as the nurse combed his hair. A line of drool glistened in the crease below his mouth, which collapsed on one side like a failed soufflé.

"He had one of his scares," the nurse said in her accented French. "He's been good

222

this morning, otherwise."

"Did he eat his eggs?" Hélène asked.

"Two," the nurse said. "He got a little on his pants, though, didn't you?" she said to Jacques. "We had to change them."

She drew the comb around Jacques's ear, raking the scalp. She smelled like talc and perspiration and had huge breasts that Jacques tried to touch sometimes. During their marriage, Jacques hadn't been much of a lover. In those years, when Hélène was young, it always felt as if he were borrowing her when she wanted to be taken. She'd been his secretary, and he'd declared his feelings by leaving a new blotter on her desk. She'd been beautiful in her twenties, tall, blond, and elegant, with a *superbe décolleté*. "You're too good for me," he said on their fourth date. For many years of their marriage, Hélène had agreed.

"I made duck confit for dinner," Hélène said to Jacques. "Your favorite."

Buried along the line of Jacques's scalp were flakes of dandruff. The nurse teased them out with the comb. Once, Hélène had watched her give him a bath from the doorway of the bathroom. The nurse ran the sponge over his shoulders and down his chest as Hélène had done when she'd cared for him.

"Your hair looks lovely, darling," Hélène said. She heard plodding steps down the hall.

"Doesn't Grandpa look nice?" She turned to Adèle. "As if he were going to church."

In the doorway, Adèle seemed terrified, and for a second Hélène could see Jacques through her eyes. He was, indeed, frightening-looking. Then again, so was she. She knew that she was not a sweet, soft grandmother. There were different kinds of wrinkles, and she had the angry ones. Lashes. The pucker of repeated frowns.

"Adèle is visiting us," Hélène told Jacques. "Manu's girl. We bought a coconut this morning at the *hypermarché,* the one off the *autoroute* that you and I don't like because it's too big. I bought steaks for lunch tomorrow there as well, all wrapped in plastic. The last time I went to Marcel's the new butcher didn't cut off enough of the fat."

Jacques closed his eyes. He burrowed his head between the nurse's breasts.

"Silly boy," the nurse said. Backing up, she smiled at Adèle. "How nice that you've come to keep your grandmother company."

"We were going to play solitaire," Hélène said. "Weren't we, Adèle?"

Adèle nodded. Hélène felt grateful. She'd

been too hard on the girl in the *hypermarché,* telling her that she must choose a fruit. She'd treated her with the kind of disdain people showed to the overweight, which was not so dissimilar to the disdain people showed to the old.

"We're off, then." She kissed Jacques on the carefully tilled top of his head.

Back in the kitchen, Adèle said, "Could we open the coconut right away? I want to try the milk. Like in *Tintin aux Antilles?*"

"You know that one, do you? Well, I don't see why not."

The book had been Emmanuel's favorite *bande dessinée.* When he was very young and Alexis was a baby, Jacques would read it to him over and over in his small bed. Jacques would take off his shoes and plump a pillow behind his head. Sometimes, after a long day at work, he would fall asleep, and Hélène left him there all night, the book open on his chest.

"Manu told me the story when I was little," Adèle said. "He said that if we ever saw a coconut we could try it."

"All right. Let's get it open. And then we could make a coconut flan. You do like flan, don't you? I suppose we could grate the flesh like cheese."

She took the plums and oranges out of

225

the fruit bowl. One thing about her, she could admit when she was wrong. Adèle hadn't been trying to be difficult when she chose the fruit. She'd simply wanted to try a coconut. Tea on the roof. The poor child. Cécile and Emmanuel had managed to convince her that what was happening now in Paris — the empty corners, the two chairs at the table rather than three — was not a catastrophe. They acted as if their lives were happening to other people in a valley whom they themselves were watching from a mountain. But she knew the winds were cold and that her son was suffering.

"Have you been happy with Jacques?" Cécile had asked Hélène once, when she was pregnant with Adèle.

"I don't ask myself that question," Hélène had said. "He's a good, kind man."

And he had been, always, until the stroke. The week that they came back from the hospital, he turned over in bed and slapped Hélène on the cheek.

"You cunt," he said. "Leave my tomatoes alone."

The next morning, as she poured his coffee, he tried to punch her in the stomach. A day later, he almost pushed her down the stairs. She caught herself on the railing. She didn't tell the boys or the nurse who came

226

afternoons, or the physical therapist. He'd pushed her again one morning when she was trying to give him his bath, and she slipped on the tile. Her hip snapped. Pain forked up her side. Jacques still in the water, she'd crawled to the phone in the hall to call the doctor. He put her on pain medication and put Jacques on sedatives. He said, "*Madame,* you need help, and I am going to arrange it for you." He patted her hand. He said, "This must be so difficult." He reminded her of Jacques. She had started to cry. Now she regretted having called him.

"Let's spread out some newspaper on the table," she told Adèle. "Your grandfather is calm again. The nurse will take him for his walk to the forest."

They examined the coconut. "I suppose we'll have to smash it with a hammer," Hélène said.

"Then the milk will spill out."

"That would be messy."

"And we'd lose all the milk."

"How did the islander open the coconut in *Tintin* to drink the milk, then?"

"I don't know. Manu didn't tell that part. He'd only say the islander opened the coconut."

Jacques had started to moan again.

"She's getting your grandfather ready for

his walk to the forest," Hélène said. "Remember how he used to take you mushrooming?" Adèle didn't answer. She looked terrified again.

Hélène took the coconut off the table and handed it to her. "I'll call your father to ask what we should do. Why don't you bring this outside? We'll open it there. Less mess that way."

Emmanuel's cell phone blared several times before he picked up.

"Oh, good," Hélène said. "You made it back safely."

"I meant to call. The phone died, and then the movers were here. How's Adèle?"

"She's fine. We bought a coconut. She said you'd told her the story of Tintin."

"Told it to her, yes. I didn't buy it for her, though. The drawings are racist."

"Really? You read it and you aren't racist."

"I'm not a lot of things I could be."

Hélène could hear men talking in the background, feet thudding under furniture. A cupboard slammed. Cécile would be taking half of the pots and the plates, the knives, forks, and spoons.

"Do you remember how they open the coconut in the book?" she asked.

"I think the islander hits it against his head."

228

"That doesn't help much," Hélène said. She paused. On the floor above, the nurse and Jacques were starting down the stairs. "Adèle says she'll be able to have tea on the roof at her mother's apartment."

"Maybe she will. You know Cécile. *Elle en est capable.*"

He still loved her, Hélène thought, despite what she'd done to him and what she kept doing. What more does she say she wants from you? Hélène wanted to ask. Passion? Adventure? Of course she had thought about whether she was happy with Jacques. Of course she'd asked herself the question that Cécile had once asked her. She'd been that age once. She'd been beautiful too, though in a more groomed way. But she could no more have this conversation with her son than she could have had that one with Cécile.

"I'm making steak for lunch tomorrow," she said. "Don't hurt your back if you help with the couch."

"Thanks, *Maman,*" Emmanuel said.

She hung up the phone. Your daughter is fat, Emmanuel, she would continue on to say. She needs to go on a diet. Cécile has left you. She knew she would leave you one day, and that's why she didn't want to have your baby. Maybe *Tintin* is racist, but that story made you happy. You would put your head on your father's shoulder as he read. You would say, "One more time, Papa. It isn't too late." Some things you have to make simple even though they aren't. You will see this when you look back after I'm dead. You will think: I'm glad I had that lunch with my father, even though he didn't recognize me and moaned all of a sudden for nothing and spit out his food. You will think, I'm glad my mother made me.

She walked down the hall, by the nurse and Jacques.

"We're off to get our fresh air," the nurse said, brightly.

"Have a good walk, darling," Hélène said to Jacques.

In the storage room, the freezer hummed and the air smelled of old onions and dirt. She looked at the boxes, stacked with her parents' wedding portrait that had hung over the fireplace when she and Jacques lived in Paris, his mother's sewing machine, a crate of Guy's few belongings sent to them after his suicide, the boys' crib mattresses like slices of bread against the wall. She opened the box labeled *Livres/Enfance* in Jacques's precise writing. Several books in, she found *Tintin aux Antilles*. She stood in the circle of light from the bulb on the ceiling.

"Let's go, Snowy," Tintin says. "We are off on a mission."

They crash on an island with shaggy palms. A red-lipped, big-eyed islander named Ratatata teaches them to make a hut from palm fronds and to spear fish. Until Captain Haddock saves them, they live off the coconuts that Ratatata opens by smacking the shell against his forehead into perfect halves.

"C'est facile, mes amis," Ratatata says.

Hélène closed the book and put it back in the box. Emmanuel had remembered correctly. She didn't know what he meant about the drawings being racist, though.

Outside, the nurse was helping Jacques along the brick path that ran past the vegetable garden that Jacques's father had started and Jacques had extended to the forest's shade. Several years back, he'd added a row of cherry trees for the grandchildren to pick. When the men from the village came to dig near the well, they found, buried in the dirt, an assortment of black market goods from the war: bars of swan-shaped soap disintegrated in their wrappings, rusted tins of *pâté,* bottles of putrid perfume and flat champagne. After

Jacques's stroke, Hélène hired the same men to pull up the plants in the vegetable garden — she couldn't bear to do it — to prevent Jacques from going through the gate to eat the leaves and roots. The fence now closed off a rectangle of dirt. Everything that had been charming about the cottage when Hélène used to visit her in-laws had evaporated. And the manor up the drive was being rented out as a *gîte rural* for American and English tourists who drove too fast and played music at night and kept knocking on the door of the cottage for directions as if this were once again the house of servants.

Adèle sat on the grass by the well, the coconut between her legs.

"No luck, I'm afraid," Hélène said. "Your papa says to give you a kiss. Have you come up with anything?"

Adèle shook her head. Her eyes were full and heavy. The girl could be pretty if she melted off some of that weight.

Hélène looked over at Jacques, who was waiting for the nurse to zip up his coat.

"We could try your grandfather," she said. Jacques's memory, the doctor had explained, was like Gruyère cheese. That was why, sometimes, rarely, he would blink, as if clearing fog from his eyes, and smile at her.

She and Adèle went over to Jacques. Hélène handed him the coconut.

"We aren't sure how to open this, darling."

Jacques looked at the coconut. He drew back his arms. Hélène thought for a moment that he might hit it against his own forehead, and, as in a fairy tale, the right side of his mouth would rise. He'd say her name in the calm, easy voice that used to irritate her. Instead, he swung the coconut between his legs and tossed it at the garden gate.

"He thinks it's a *pétanque* ball, perhaps," the nurse said.

"He didn't play *pétanque*," Hélène said.

She hated the nurse suddenly: her breasts, her smile, her helpfulness, her accent, the way Jacques held on to her hand. The coconut had rolled into a gatepost, under the raspberry brambles. Adèle fished it out.

"He could have broken it," she said, as Jacques and the nurse started down the path toward the forest.

"He wouldn't have meant to," Hélène said. Jacques stumbled and the nurse lifted his arm over her shoulders.

"Is that Grandpa's girlfriend?" Adèle asked.

"I don't know," Hélène said. "And I don't know how we will open that coconut."

"We could look it up," Adèle said.

She had to buy Adèle a second ice cream at the *glacerie,* but she told her to choose a sorbet this time. They sat at the same table. Adèle typed the words with her thumbs: How do you open a coconut? Hélène moved her chair closer so she could watch too. A tiny movie played — a black man sat on a beach with a coconut. He explained that the first thing one should do was to empty the water from the coconut to make opening it easier.

"Water," Hélène said. "We thought it was milk."

"These are the eyes," the man said. He took a screwdriver and knocked the tip into the brown circles with a hammer. Then he drained the coconut into a bowl. He tapped the equator around the coconut, and it split into two perfect halves.

"He makes it look so easy," Hélène said.

Back home, she went to the closet where Jacques had urinated that morning and took a screwdriver from the toolbox on the shelf.

"I was your grandfather's secretary, you know," she told Adèle when she was back at the kitchen table. "I made his appointments. That's how we met. And we stayed together all this time. Once, we delivered a baby together on the Métro."

Adèle held the coconut between her knees.

They took turns twisting the screwdriver into the eye of the coconut. The train had been stuck in a tunnel for a half hour already when the woman started to moan. Jacques had told the passengers at the back to please move to the front of the car. "You hold her legs," he said to Hélène. "It will be fine," he told the woman. "We've done this before. Two healthy boys. Listen to my count. Push when I tell you." The woman's knees shook. She cried and moaned.

"That's one," Adèle said. She started on the other eye. The shell chipped under the blade. Hélène put her hands in her lap and watched.

The truth is, Emmanuel, she would say, if that woman hadn't cried out at the stop between Bonne Nouvelle and Saint-Ambroise, maybe your parents wouldn't have stayed together. Maybe your mother, like Cécile, would have decided to flee, the mother you think you know so well that you don't need to stay for her coffee and palmiers. But your father, Emmanuel, the way he stood up in that train and went to that woman. The way he knew I would follow. I saw him again for the first time that day. And that was enough.

"Done," Adèle said.

"Keep it upright," Hélène said. "Don't let

any spill out."

From the cupboard, she took two champagne glasses. The water sloshed down the sides of the coconut as she poured.

"It doesn't taste very good," Adèle said after taking a sip.

"No," Hélène said. "It doesn't."

Jacques and the nurse had returned from the walk. He leaned on her arm, shuffling down the hall. Hélène took another sip. She wondered if he had ever played *pétanque*. She wondered if he'd known the secret to opening a coconut once. She wondered, as he passed by the kitchen and saw that old woman and that plump girl, who he thought they were.

ANTS

2009

From the boat, Adèle watched the last passenger — an old man in a straw hat — make his way along the reef. He stopped and bent down, feet amputated by the ocean. Twice since he'd left the beach, he had slipped his hand into the water, pulled out a shell, and put it in the bag that hung from his shoulder. This one, a flash of sunlight in his palm, looked smaller than the others, the home of a tiny creature with legs like a spider or the gooey foot of a snail. He stood up and continued to wade toward the dock where the boat was moored, his face lost in the shadow of his hat. He didn't seem to be in a hurry, although the islander, a long man with tattoos of turtles and spears on his chest, had waved to him twice and now straddled the bow, chewing betel nut and spitting the juice overboard.

The boat, a motorized version of a pirogue

237

canoe, shifted with the tide so that the islander looked as if he were balancing on a seesaw, and the passengers tilted into each other. On the bench across from Adèle, her father, Emmanuel, was rolling a cigarette, and her mother, Cécile, was talking to a Belgian woman who had a soft, round face fit for a *boulangerie* counter, and a Roquefort marbling of varicose veins on her legs. Or rather, the Belgian woman was talking to Cécile. She and her husband came to this resort every winter, she said, she to collapse on the beach and her husband to play golf and tennis. They found Tahiti to be the most beautiful former colony and the natives the friendliest. Had Cécile tried the spa? The guava facial was *incroyable.*

"No," Cécile said, *"mais ça a l'air délicieux."*

She was humoring the Belgian woman with her interested expression — eyes squinting, chin tilted — round face framed by her cropped hair above her bony ballerina torso. But Adèle knew what her mother was thinking: *Quelle idiote.* The Belgian couple — the only other people on this snorkeling excursion save the islander and the old man — wore Lacoste collared shirts, and shorts that went to their knees. They lived in Poitiers, "not in the city itself," the woman had said. Their two children were grown now; the girl went to an *école de commerce,* and the boy was studying *l'économie.* The man called his wife *"chérie."* He wore a gold necklace. She had a bright, eager laugh that shot out from her mouth and hit you in the face. They were deep bourgeois, the kind of people Adèle's parents disdained, people who owned shops and voted UMP.

"Are you excited to see the fish?" the Belgian woman said to Adèle. "They are supposed to be *extraordinaires.*"

"Yes," Adèle said. "Very."

She felt from the Belgian woman's frozen smile that she'd answered the question incorrectly. When she was little, she could say anything as dull as "I'll have the *steak frites,* please," or "I'm in second year at school," and adults would find her brilliant because she was big-eyed and plump and had freckles on the bridge of her nose. Then she stopped being little, and adults looked away or seemed to be indulging her by listening. Since she'd turned thirteen, risen a meter, and grown tiny humps on her chest, things had changed again. Men joked with her now, and women stood back a little. If Adèle had felt more comfortable with children, if she had more friends, she would not talk to adults at all.

"If he doesn't hurry up, we might never leave for the island to see those extraordinary fish." Cécile looked out at the old man. The Belgian woman drew back on the bench. Cécile had repeated *"extraordinaires"* with a high, mocking intonation. She knew how to pull people in and then cast them aside. Despite saying that she was interested in differences, she grew bored easily in the conversations she struck up with the man at the *épicerie* or with Adèle's teachers. It had been a revelation to Adèle to see that her mother acted this way. More and more, lately, she had these sudden ideas that sprouted in her brain and kept growing until she felt her head would explode. It was, she knew, part of growing up. And she didn't like it. She didn't see what good could come from knowing the flaws in her parents' characters and in their relationship. It wasn't *normal* to live together and then live apart and then live together again. It wasn't *normal* to have boyfriends and girlfriends, as the "friends" her parents referred to were. All this might be Cécile and Emmanuel's way of doing things, but it was not *normal,* although Adèle wasn't sure what *normal* was, exactly.

"Here," Emmanuel said to Cécile.

"Smoke. It'll relax you."

"Do I not seem relaxed?" She took the cigarette. "How could a person not be relaxed in a place like this?"

She had started to criticize the resort as soon as they got out of the airport bus, when a woman in a grass skirt hung hibiscus leis around their necks and welcomed them to paradise.

"Yes, of course," Cécile said as they rolled their suitcases along the path to their room, past a pool shaped like a lima bean. "In paradise, brown people serve white people."

"S'il te plaît," Emmanuel said. "We said we'd try."

"You said we'd try."

Adèle had slowed her pace to fall behind them. There they went again. When she was younger, she would put her ear to the door of her bedroom to grab at words and try to make sense of what they were saying. She didn't anymore. It was always the same fight, anyway. Something about money, or Cécile being harsh, or Emmanuel being controlling. Nothing ever changed. Six months ago, Adèle's grandfather, Jacques, had died. Cécile and Emmanuel had been living separately for years, but at the funeral in Benneville, Cécile stroked Emmanuel's ponytail as he cried, and a few weeks later she moved back in. For a while, things were calm, even pleasant, and then the fighting restarted. When Emmanuel got his inheritance, he said that they should spend it on a vacation together. Cécile had been enthusiastic until she wasn't.

"Mind rolling me one too?" the Belgian man asked.

"*Tu vas fumer?*" his wife said.

He shrugged. "When in Rome."

Cécile cupped her hand around the cigarette to light it and then handed it to the Belgian man. Emmanuel rolled her another one. Adèle turned back around to watch the old man, who had almost reached the boat. That morning, as her parents had fought in the room, she'd wandered outside. Clouds cocooned the mountain above, a dormant volcano set in glossy jungle. The resort stretched along the cliff in a pattern of wooden houses with thatched roofs and porches, to a main building decorated with tapa cloth and ceremonial fly whisks, past the pool, tennis courts, and, oddly, a chapel. The air was swampy, steamy, and sweet. The coconut trees that sprouted from the grass were a disappointment. The resort cut down the nuts so they wouldn't fall on the heads of the guests. Adèle yanked a banana from a tree and sent it spinning like a boomerang over the edge of the cliff. It was then that she saw the old man on the reef. He walked bent over, face down, as if he were reading the coral.

She was reminded of her grandfather Jacques, before his stroke. He would take her out mushrooming when she visited Benneville. She held the basket and he walked like that, stooped over, shuffling through the oak leaves and needles. This is a *chanterelle,* he would say. This is a *cèpe.* This one is poisonous — you can tell from the tightness of the gills. He let her cut the stalks and put the mushrooms in the basket. Her grandfather Jacques was gentle and sweet, and then he was dead, even though he was still alive. A month after his funeral, Adèle had taken the train to Benneville by herself to visit her grandmother Hélène, who met her at the station dressed for church, her leather handbag on her arm. "I thought we would visit your grandfather," she said, after kissing Adèle on the cheeks. It was the season of the Fête du Muguet so, once they'd put Adèle's suitcase in the car, they bought a bouquet of lilies of the valley from a stand in the square and walked to the cemetery. Grandfather Jacques's grave, a square of dirt when Adèle last saw it, now had a marble slab and a headstone.

"You see how it matches your great-grandparents' and your great-uncle Guy's headstones exactly," her grandmother Hélène said. She pointed at a bare spot of grass near the wall that encircled the cemetery. "And I'll go over there when it's my turn. It's as close as I can get." She laid the bouquet of *muguet* on the slab. "I'd like chrysanthemums on mine, please. The pompom kind. You'll remember that, won't you?"

"D'accord," Adèle said. She was growing sick to her stomach at the thought of her grandfather Jacques under that slab and wanted to go. But her grandmother snapped open the purse she'd set by her feet and took out a bag of Haribo marshmallow bears. *"Ton bonbon préféré,"* she said. "I made a special trip to the *tabac* for these." She opened the bag and held it out for Adèle. "Eat one before they melt in this heat."

Adèle didn't want a marshmallow bear — she liked the gummies — plus she wanted to get away from the grave and out of the cemetery. But she took a bear and bit off its head. Her grandmother Hélène seemed satisfied. They stood there for a moment, looking at the headstone, the marshmallow suffocating Adèle's tongue, and then Hélène said, "I've learned something about your grandfather Jacques. I'll tell your parents and uncle at Christmas, when everyone is together. But I wanted you to know first. Because you are my favorite. And knowing first is one of the advantages of being the favorite." She took a small, quick breath. "At your grandfather's funeral," she said, "before we all left the church for the meal, a man named Marcel came up to me. You wouldn't know him. He was the village butcher for years and years. He said that he wanted to tell me something about your grandfather and asked that I come visit him in his nursing home. So, last week, I did. We sat in the garden. He's old as a prune but sharp as a pencil." Hélène touched Adèle's shoulder. "You should finish that before it gets all over your hands." Adèle put the rest of the bear in her mouth.

"Your great-grandfather Henri," Hélène continued, "as you know, was in the resistance in Benneville during the war. Well, more than in the resistance. He *was* the resistance. He and Marcel. They organized everything." One night, she went on, not long after the German occupation, Henri came to the back door of the *boucherie* and told Marcel that the nuns at the convent up

the road from Benneville had been de-
nounced to the Gestapo for hiding refugees.
There would be a raid on the convent the
next morning. Henri and Marcel went
through the forest to the convent. They led
the families hiding there to the Seine, where
another man took them into his fishing
boat, covered them with a tarp, and floated
them to safety. Henri and Marcel urged the
nuns to escape down the Seine too, but they
refused to leave. "There was a newborn
baby at the convent that they'd been caring
for," Hélène said, "the child of an unwed
mother. According to Marcel, your great-
grandfather Henri took that baby home.
Your great-grandmother was eight months
pregnant with your uncle, Guy, at the time.
So when Guy was born, the boys were only
six weeks apart, close enough to be taken
for fraternal twins." Hélène looked down at
Adèle. "Do you understand?"

"Yes," Adèle said. "Grandfather Jacques's
mother and father weren't his mother and
father."

"Exactly." Hélène took a handkerchief
from the sleeve of her blouse and gave it to
Adèle. Adèle wiped the invisible chocolate
from her fingers.

"The nuns were arrested the next morning and taken away. So all these years,

nobody knew this story except for your great-grandparents and Marcel, who promised to keep quiet. Your great-grandparents didn't want Jacques to feel that he wasn't truly part of the family, or for him to be gossiped about. He'd have been called a bastard back then. He still would be today by some. Not everyone is as comfortable as your parents with children being born out of wedlock, you know." Hélène held out her hand for the handkerchief, then folded it back into her sleeve. "I suppose when I tell everyone, your mother will find this all very ironic. And your father. Well, who knows what he'll think. I can never predict. The only thing I'm sure of is that I will have done something wrong. If I were to tell them now, they'd say I should have waited for them to finish grieving. When I tell them at Christmas, they'll say I should have told them now." She sighed. "What do you think?"

"I think it was very kind of him," Adèle said.

Hélène looked confused. "Of whom?"

"My great-grandfather Henri. Everyone says he was mean." Emmanuel and Cécile called him a tyrant, and Hélène herself had once told Adèle that her great-grandfather Henri had a chestnut for a heart.

"He *was* mean," Hélène said. "And it wouldn't have been kindness that made him take your grandfather home. Henri wanted to *see* himself as someone who would take an abandoned baby home. It's different. Anyway, I meant what do you think about how your parents and your uncle will react to this news. Badly, no?"

"Probably," Adèle said, not sure what answer her grandmother wanted, exactly, but knowing by the way she picked up her purse and said they should get home that she had once again said the wrong thing.

The islander helped the old man into the boat.

"Maeva," he said, using the Tahitian word for hello. "Forgive me for holding you up. I can't be on a reef and not look."

"We noticed," Cécile said. She smiled loosely.

"Looks like you're doing well," the Belgian woman said. She'd tucked herself under her husband's hairy arm, shifting back to avoid the streams of smoke from his mouth.

"I found a couple good ones." The old man sat down next to Adèle. He settled the bag between his ankles. His toenails were thick and hoary and grew over the edges of his toes. In the bag between his ankles, something clicked. A shape rose like a tens-

ing muscle under the canvas, and then disappeared.

"*On y va,*" the islander said. "Look for
dolphins." The island, he told them, pointing, was that line on the horizon.

"Tell me if you see something," Emmanuel
said to Adèle.

"I will," Adèle said. But she wasn't looking for dolphins. When the boat started to
cut over the water and the adults on the
other bench turned to watch, she said to
the old man, "I saw you out there this
morning, as well. You found something big."

The old man smiled. The skin pleated
around his eyes.

"Something big and extraordinary. Do
you want to see?"

Adèle nodded. He opened the bag. With
both hands, he took out the shell. It was as
full and heavy as a melon, the outside
chalky, the inside a smooth and glistening
pink. From the cliff it had resembled a ball
of light.

"They don't get much rarer than this," he
said. "I've been coming here for years and
years, longer than you've been alive. This is
the first one I've found."

He dug a bent finger into the slit where
the two sides of the shell came together.
"The mollusk's got its operculum closed.

That's its trapdoor." He wiped his finger on the leg of his shorts.

"Crazy that you can walk out there and find something like that," Emmanuel said over the sound of the engine.

"*Je crois que c'est une espèce protégée,*" the islander said.

"No one minds," the old man said. He lifted the shell out of Adèle's hands and put it back in the bag.

No dolphins had appeared on the way to the island, which was shaggy with palms, which gave way to beach, which gave way to ocean, which gave way to reef. They laid their towels on the sand. The islander took out a small grill and cooler from the boat. He cut open a mango and gave everyone a slice.

"Let's go in." Emmanuel opened the bag of snorkeling gear.

"Don't feel like it yet." Cécile pulled off her shirt and undid her bikini top.

"Isn't that why we did this? *Pour voir des poissons?*"

"See the fish if you want," Cécile said. "I'm not stopping you."

Emmanuel got that look on his face. Cécile sat down on her towel. Adèle saw the Belgian man gaze in her direction. Her mother had beautiful breasts, like the ones on the women in the paintings at the Louvre, as round and full as moons, with raspberry nipples.

"*Allez,* Adèle," Emmanuel said. "*On y va.*"

"She just ate," Cécile said. "You're supposed to wait a half hour."

"She had one piece of mango."

"You're her father. If you think it's safe, I guess it is."

"Fine," Emmanuel said, and then added to Adèle, "Come when you're ready."

He stalked off, toward the water. They did this to her all the time, whether they were living together or not. Adèle had been a vegetarian for a while because her mother looked so pained when she ate meat with Emmanuel, and then she'd started to eat meat again, because he said it was no fun having a charcuterie plate on your own. They'd go to museums together, and he'd say he liked the modernists, whereas Cécile would say she liked the more contemporary art, and then they'd both look at Adèle. This trip had started out that way too. Emmanuel wanted to go to Tahiti and Cécile wanted to go to Martinique. They'd made Adèle decide. "You have the right to as much of an opinion as we do," they were always saying, but she always felt as if she were choosing incorrectly.

Adèle watched Emmanuel fade down the line of turquoise water as the air sharpened with the smell of the heating coals from the grill. The old man was farther down the beach. Behind him, the sky stretched like a sheet of rubber pulled tight, light on top, dark at the bottom.

"Where's Manu going?" Adèle said.

"You know him," Cécile said. "He needs to stomp a little." She turned to the Belgian man. "*Je le punis*. He shouldn't have told me to relax."

The Belgian man smiled. "I can tell you keep him on his toes."

He dug his elbows into the sand. His wife had fallen asleep on her towel, the cover of her book on her face. Adèle lay back on her towel and closed her eyes. Sometimes it was easier to play dead. Her face felt warm and nice in the sun, and the beach cradled her back. She heard the rustle of sand as the Belgian man shifted closer to Cécile. His body was thicker than Emmanuel's. Adèle had seen her father naked often in the bathroom and on the beach, although he'd stopped walking around that way since he'd caught her staring at that strange elephant trunk that was a penis. When Adèle had turned ten, Cécile told her everything, about a man putting his penis into you, how it got hard, about how men and women used their tongues and stuck fingers into each other, and when Adèle said, "Even in their butt holes?" Cécile took a puff of her pipe and said yes, and gay men put their penises there as well. There was no reason to be puritanical about sex. It was fun and natural, though you did need to take some precautions. Girls needed to know what was what, she said. And Adèle shouldn't let any man touch her until she was ready. If a man tried to do that, she must tell Cécile. Some men thought they had a right to take any-thing they wanted. It was a *problème d'évolution.* While the men had been off hunting animals, the women had been in the caves, thinking. That was why women were more evolved intellectually and emo-tionally, and why men still acted like hunters.

"We aren't great at doing nothing to-gether," Cécile said. "And the resort is a little too pretty for me."

"It used to be a leper colony, you know," the Belgian man said.

"Sérieusement?"

"Says so on a plaque by the tennis courts. It's their dirty secret. Play a match with me. I'll show you."

"I haven't in years, not since I was a kid. We live in Trocadéro now. Not many courts around there."

"It's not something you forget how to do. I'd like a new partner. The resort pro beats me every time."

"I'd beat you too. Don't underestimate me."

Adèle opened her eyes and got up from the towel. "I think it's okay to go in now," she said.

"D'accord," Cécile said. "I'll be in soon. Did you put on sunscreen?"

"Yes," Adèle said. "This morning while I was waiting for you and Manu."

"Don't be pouty," Cécile said.

Adèle walked out of the tobacco smell and into the smell of roasting meat from the grill. Her eyes stung and she blinked hard until the sky and the ocean came back into focus. The islander was in the boat, hauling out the cooler. Emmanuel was still walking down the beach.

The old man had opened his bag on the sand and was sorting through the shells. When one of them trundled away, he grabbed it and put it on its back in the pile. Inside the slit, claws wiggled and churned.

"How do you get the animal out of the shell?" Adèle asked.

"Come by my hut later. I'll show you."

"I don't know if I can."

"You seem resourceful."

"Where is it?" she said, and he told her. *"D'accord,"* she said. "I'll try."

She walked into the water until she was up to her waist and the warmth was woven through with cold. She pulled the mask over her eyes. She started by floating, and then kicked her way out. She felt disappointed until she saw a clownfish, followed by another. She lifted her head out of the water. Cécile and the Belgian man were putting on snorkeling masks in the tide. She took a breath of rubber-flavored air and went under again. Inky urchins and bouquets of seaweed studded the ocean floor. A school of angelfish parted in front of her face. Their eyes were flat and black. So many pretty things weren't pretty up close. She'd caught a butterfly once in her grandfather's garden and found its face hideous. Now her grandfather was under a slab of marble, his hair and nails still growing, cheeks caving in. Once, he'd been a baby, and her great-grandfather Henri had taken him in his arms and brought him home and chosen to be his father. No matter what her grandmother Hélène said, or what Emmanuel and Cécile and her uncle, Alexis, and her aunt, Kate, said when they learned this story at Christmas, no matter what the story meant to anyone else about who Jacques had been or who they themselves were or thought they had been, Adèle knew one thing: her great-grandfather Henri had been kind. She had never even met him, and she might be the only person who understood this about him.

A wave crashed over her back. Water poured into the snorkel. She lifted her head to spit. Cécile and the Belgian man bobbed nearby. Back under the surface, a cloud of parrot fish scattered in a fluorescent blur. After following them for a few strokes, she let her body go slack. She opened her arms as if she were flying. She turned. Cécile and the Belgian man floated over a turban of coral. He was pointing at a cluster of anemones, Adèle saw as she drew closer, flame-orange, tentacles fluttering. Cécile slipped deeper and swirled her index finger along the tentacles.

Adèle pushed out the snorkel with her tongue. The sound of her own screaming came at her through the thud of the waves and the thick water. She kicked toward Cécile.

"*Requin,*" she yelled.

Above the jerking waves, Cécile grabbed

her hand. The Belgian man had heard and was heading for the shore. Adèle and Cécile swam side by side, Cécile kicking, tugging at Adèle's arm. The urchins appeared, then the seaweed. A pair of arms lifted Adèle from the water and she saw the islander's legs and chest. He carried her out of the foam, set her down gently on her feet and, as she caught her breath, undid the seal on her mask with his thumbs.

"Calme-toi, ma petite," he said. "Sharks don't come in that close. It must have been something else you saw."

The Belgian man kneeled in the sand, panting. Cécile had staggered up to them, welts from the mask on her forehead and cheeks. She kissed Adèle on the mouth.

"Merde," she said. "That was scary."

The Belgian woman stood next to her husband with her hand on his shoulder.

"You're a brave girl," she said to Adèle. "Good thing you were out there with them."

The old man wasn't back from combing the beach, but the rest of them ate the grilled pork wrapped in cassava leaves. Adèle sat next to Emmanuel, who had returned after they'd all dried off. Cécile wasn't speaking to him, because she said he was supposed to have been in the water with Adèle. As they ate lunch, he kept reaching out to run his hand down the back of Adèle's head.

"If it was a shark, it was a leopard shark," he said. "It wouldn't have hurt you."

"Still," Cécile said. "It was a shark."

"It bumped my leg, I think," the Belgian man said.

"You come to a place like this," his wife said, "and you think nothing bad can happen."

When they'd finished eating, the Belgian man followed his wife to the boat as Adèle and Emmanuel collected their books and towels. Cécile was rinsing the sand off their snorkeling gear at the edge of the water.

"Je suis désolé," Emmanuel said. "Cécile's right. I was pissed off. I should have been out there with you. Vacations are hard. Too many compromises to make. But it's good for a couple to have differences, you know. You'll see that as you get older."

Ahead, Cécile was climbing into the boat with the help of the Belgian man. When they returned to Paris, Adèle knew, she would move back to her apartment. Adèle would eat steak with Emmanuel one night and vegetable patties with Cécile the next. She'd go with him and his "friends" to jazz concerts and with her and her "friends" to protests at city hall. She'd sleep under the blanket at Emmanuel's apartment one night and the duvet at Cécile's apartment another. She'd get dressed before coming out of her bedroom for breakfast so that she wouldn't meet whoever was in this kitchen or that kitchen in her pajamas. Things would be *normal* again.

"Cécile wants to play tennis," she told Emmanuel. "She said so while you were gone."

"Cécile plays tennis?"

"She did when she was a kid."

"Then why don't you two play? I was thinking I'd go see the volcano, and she doesn't want to."

"I don't know how." Adèle pointed at the boat. "But he does."

The ocean hit the beach, drawing in grains of sand. The shark rose again, this time into the air, made of sand instead of seaweed, circling her mother and the Belgian man.

The old man's bungalow was easy to find, nestled in plumeria trees next to the tennis courts. He was on the porch, laying shells on their backs. He stood up as Adèle climbed the steps. Without his hat, under a thin veil of hair, his scalp was splotched and peeling.

"You came," he said. "I hoped you would."

He pointed at a shell. "*Tu vois?* They do the work for me."

Adèle kneeled down to look. Bits of flesh on their backs, the ants moved in a line from the inside of the shell, dropped off the side of the porch into the grass, and then filed back for more.

The Mouth of the Ocean sat alone at the top of the stairs. "Can I hold it again?" she asked.

"It's not done yet."

"I don't care."

The old man gave her the shell. The ants spilled over the sides and onto her arm in a tickling stream. The old man didn't move his hand away. Slowly, he ran his finger along the edge of Adèle's thumb.

"Beautiful, isn't it?" he said.

Beyond his shoulder, on the lawn, Cécile and the Belgian man were walking toward the tennis courts with their rackets. The ants crept over the shallow of Adèle's elbow, up into her armpit.

"Oui," she said.

"Let's go inside. There's more I could show you."

Cécile and the Belgian man were almost at the tennis courts now. Adèle walked to the edge of the porch. She held up the shell.

"Look!" she shouted. "Look what he gave me."

BETWEEN

Is it always or?
Is it never and?
  — Stephen Sondheim, *Into the Woods*

AND

Tonight, we sit at a table in your cottage
with my husband and your wife, passing the
cornichons, the pâté, the butter that you
and I use on our bread. Through the window, my daughters play in your garden.
They swat cherries off the trees with bad-
minton racquets and then dig them out of
the grass. Your son, visiting from Provence,
watches from a bench with his girlfriend,
who is holding my baby in her lap. Your
children, my children. His children. Her
children.

During the first course, your wife and my
husband speak French, as you and I slide
into English. The four of us discuss the train
that the two of them catch each Friday

when they return to Benneville from Paris, which you and I — implanted here all summer — don't need to escape.

"You okay?" you ask as my husband helps your wife to bring in the main course. You say my name as my teachers in Syracuse used to say it, making Élodie sound like Melody. I nod, yes, yes, why wouldn't I be? But my eyes tell your dimming eyes, No, I'm not. I hate your boots by the front door. I hate the foxgloves on the table arranged by your wife. I hate the soap in the bathroom worn down by four hands.

You take a sip of wine. I lose your gaze behind the rim of the glass.

"You're quieter than usual," you say. "Not used to that."

"Your cat has my tongue." It's been slinking between my feet since I sat down. "I didn't think of you as a cat person."

The truth is, I'm hurt that you never mentioned you had one.

"I'm not," you say. "I like dogs."

And that's all it takes. When they come back into the room, we're talking about the dogs we had as children. A black Lab and a beagle, breeds that are uncommon here.

He sets the roast chicken on the table. You say you'll carve and go to the buffet for a knife. I see your wife hesitate.

"The habits of surgeons die hard," she says. She watches you navigate the room, past the white brick of the fireplace. You don't put out your hand to follow the edge of the table. How long will that last? I want to give her a hug. I also want to strangle her.

You stand at the head of the table to carve. The chicken sits on a silver plate (a wedding present? You've been married almost as long as I've existed). Your index finger rides the dull edge of the knife. Not long ago, you parted skin and split breastbone to reveal a pulsing heart. With tools sized for fairies, you funneled through arteries. You created new routes around the dead ends of blockages. Now your hand holds the leg bone while the other hand slices. You keep your face to the side so that you can see better.

"Who wants the wishbone?" you ask in French, and I know you mean that it's for me. Everything I say tonight will be for you, too.

Your wife asks me about the work I'm doing on the manor. I talk about flooring, about the oak boards I am trying to find of the same width that the Légers would have walked years before my grandparents did. I tell her about the old photographs I've found in the village archives. A beautiful woman in a billowing dress, standing on the front steps next to a man with a mustache. A gardener with a wide hat, pruning the roses.

"I knew what to do with the pergola based on that photograph," I explain. And I knew to look for a lion head knocker based on the photograph of the couple. "Mostly, though, it's a lot of guesswork."

"We want to return the manor to its original splendor," my husband says, "before it was plundered," as if the memory of that splendor were in his blood, not mine. "We want our own grandchildren to live there one day."

I see you listening to him politely and I know you are thinking what he doesn't know, though he should, because he's almost forty. Things go wrong. A car runs off the road into a tree. A train derails. The macula degenerates. A cell in your bloodstream forks the wrong way. My husband's sureness, which I once loved, now embarrasses me. Sitting back, he tells you the story of the set of nesting dolls that my mother found in the manor, back when it was a ruin. He explains how he told me if one object had survived, there must be others. "I sent her off looking," he says. "I told her to find her grandparents' furniture and to buy it all back." He describes how I found their clock in the village hall. And an armchair in someone's attic. The green silk cover had been eaten away by bugs, and it had to be restuffed. "Inside the pillow had been filled with her grandparents' money."

I've already told you this story, and I watch your face open as if you are hearing it for the first time.

"Incroyable," your wife says.

"It was worth nothing now," I say.

"But you must have been glad that no one had found it," you say, as you've said before on a path by the pond.

Now your wife is asking how we met, and my husband is telling you both his version of the story, with the jokes. He went to the U.S. wanting an American business degree and ended up with an American wife, "although not a real one." You don't laugh along with your wife, because you know the feeling of not being quite this or that. I think you can tell that I'm being put down, although in my husband's teasing way. And now he is being tender again. He switches so quickly, it's hard to see. "When we got married," he says, "the manor was being rented out. Her parents couldn't afford to keep it up anymore, but they held on to it for years by the skin of their teeth. We're going to fly them here to stay for a summer once the work is done. We want to surprise them."

"First we'll have to empty the liquor cabinet," I add, and then say to your wife, because you already know: "My father is an alcoholic."

"I'd love to see what you've done," your wife says. I say, *"Bien sûr,"* but that the rooms are a mess right now, because the painters are prepping the trim. I can barely stand to be in your house, and I don't want your wife in mine. She serves me another slice of meat and hands me the bowl of sauce. Those are *trompettes de la mort,* she says, mixed into the gravy. "He found them yesterday on one of his walks."

But your walks are our walks, and we found them together, under a tussle of oak leaves. I say it's a good thing you know what you're doing, since usually Americans can't tell a poisonous mushroom from a button mushroom. You laugh and ask if I'm any better. This is our first mutual lie.

"Don't even attempt it," my husband tells me, and I laugh too.

She turns to you as you pour more wine into her glass. Do you remember, she asks, the time that the two of you ate wild mushrooms on that walk in the Alps and spent the rest of the day in bed?

"A nurse and a doctor," she says, "and we couldn't do anything for ourselves."

I try to think of you and her lying in bed, throwing up, although I'm not sure if that's what she means. She looks so intently at you that I wonder whether in fact she's looking at me.

OR

And why would you notice? He's twenty years older than we are and he can barely see. If you'd met him some years ago, when he implanted the world's first artificial heart at a hospital in Paris, you would have paid attention. Now, though, he's nothing to you. After they bought the cottage from Madame Havre's sons, you wanted to be sure that they knew about the historical zoning. Once his wife reassured you there'd be no additions, you were done with both of them. I had to tell you his name three times when I brought him up the next day. "Stephen came by for the name of a plumber."

"Who?" you said. "Oh, him. The American neighbor."

I can look through your eyes and take in his gray hair and the stoop to his shoulders that I find endearing. He has the posture of a less accomplished man, the result of so much leaning.

That morning I was in the rose garden, pruning, while the nanny watched the girls run around in the topiary and the baby slept in the shade. I felt that restlessness I'd been feeling since I finished restoring the garden and moved on to the house, maybe because I know when the house is finished there'll be nothing left to do. The garden is exactly as I wanted it to be, and it's a disappointment. I miss the fungus on the chestnut tree, now hidden by the tree house ladder. The topiary was more interesting when I didn't recognize the shapes and could see what I wanted in the bushes. The roses were more beautiful when they flared from a storm of vines and nettles, and with the wisteria clipped, the creepers and ivy cut away, the pergola looks like a cage. I haven't told you, but I've stopped looking for the missing statues of the muses. I prefer to think of them in desert gardens, by a more interesting fountain, on the steps to a beach. Anywhere but here.

"Bonjour," he called from the side of the house, and I knew the accent.

"Hello," I said. I lifted my sunglasses off my face so as not to be rude. He kept his on, because he needs them.

"Bad eyes," he explained. And then: Where are you from? How long have you lived here? He said that he didn't hear a hint of an accent when I spoke English, and I said that he would hear it if I spoke French.

"You can't be perfect in two languages," I told him. "Or at least, I can't be."

After I got him the plumber's number, I asked if he wanted a Coke float.

"You're kidding," he said.

"Le Coca et glace à la vanille," I said. "I was going to make them for the girls. I even have the straws."

We sat in the courtyard while the girls drank their floats in the tree house and the nanny took the baby for a walk on the drive. He grew up in 1970s San Francisco to my 1990s upstate New York, but over here the coasts blend, as does time.

"What did you miss most when you moved to France?" I asked, and he said, "Cheesecake."

"For me it's pickles," I said. "Cornichons are not the same thing."

I explained how I'd grown up between two countries, wanting to feel more French because my parents were French, wanting to be American because that's what I was. I told him about the American au pair, Bri-

270

gitte, who taught me English the year that I was sick, and about the stories she invented that took place in the forest. "So my first words in English were fairytale words, like *ogre* and *witch*."

"Good place to start," he said.

I described that year of my illness, and how my mother got me through it, and how, all those years when I was growing up, she would sit on the sidelines of my soccer games and go to PTA meetings. "She tried to be American for me," I said. "And then I ended up marrying a Frenchman and living in France."

He said his sons spoke English, but it was British English they'd learned in school.

"The *ou* instead of *o*," he said. *"Lorry* instead of *bus."*

"I don't even bother speaking English to my daughters," I told him. "They'll be one hundred percent French, like their father."

He said, as he left, looking up at the balcony, "I bet you're doing wonders to that house." He made it a wonder, the thing I am doing, to take something bland and make it beautiful again. He knew what I needed after an hour of conversation, whereas you don't understand even when I tell you flat out.

Hear me again: This isn't enough. And I

271

don't care anymore that it should be. You talk often about the complexity of systems. A good businessman has to see through chaos to make a decision. Why, then, have you made me so simple? And why, for so long, have I accepted your theory?

Here's all it is, though it feels like everything. Afternoons, when you're gone, I leave the children with the nanny. I turn my back to the house. The forest parts for me as a rib cage once parted for him. My body is mine. I can feel every tendon. My mind is as big as the sky, only suggested by glimpses. I understand nothing and I understand everything. And there he is, at the edge of the pond, always first, never late. It isn't me going to him, you see: it's us coming together. We circulate from separate trails.

Two and a half billion times the human heart beats in an average lifetime, pushing blood through the arteries. Connected together, the veins that receive this blood could be wrapped twice around Earth. The heart, contrary to popular belief, is not located on the left side of the body but in the middle of the chest. I know these facts because I looked them up on your computer. When you want to restore a historic house correctly, you need to learn about what it once was. And when you want to know a person, you need to understand what they love.

AND

I can't stand this yearning.

OR

Do you remember yearning?

AND

Everything you say is interesting, even when it isn't. Everything is soap opera dialogue. Like you: There are millions of stars here at night. And me: In Paris you can't see anything. And you: They're there, though, even if you can't see them. Our conversation is like the trim of the manor that the painters are scraping. Layer upon layer beneath the visible surface. Today, as we head out on a logging road, you tell me that your son has broken up with his girlfriend and is miserable.

"Love hurts," I say, and you say, "Tell me about it."

My body moves casually next to yours, but my brain orders my adrenal gland to secrete adrenaline, epinephrine, and norepinephrine. My heart beats faster than it should at this pace.

We're cutting through pine trees and oak

trees and there's no one but us. There's no country, no time, no spouses. We could be walking a forest in Massachusetts, China, or Lapland. The world is the same in the end, when you boil it down to this: two people talking on a trail. And that unnecessary hand you held out today when I jumped down from a log. I was okay but I took it.

You've told me that there are hearts that go bad for clear reasons, and hearts that go bad for reasons no one can explain. There is no clear reason why in that small exchange behind my house, I attached myself to you. Was it hearing my other language and being able to speak it? Was it the way you knew how to use a straw? Was it because I'd felt since the first workman pulled up the first vinyl tile in the kitchen that it was I who owned that house, that forest, that pond, those trails? And so, when you wandered in, I owned you?

I thought about you that week we first met, as I flipped through books of silk wallpaper samples, sent from the factory in Lyon that continues to make *les soies Léger.* They found the original order for the manor, and there were fleurs-de-lys on peacock blue for the parlor, the gold for the dining room, the red for the entryway.

Then the doorbell rang and your wife

stood behind the door. It was raining, one of those downpours we've been caught in twice. When I asked her in, she said that she didn't want to impose. She'd like to invite my husband and me to a cocktail party for a couple from Paris.

"My husband mentioned that you like painting," she said. "Our friend teaches *les arts plastiques.*"

"We'd love to," I said.

You see how we were using them already, though it didn't yet feel wrong?

At that party, after we'd talked for a while, you introduced me to the guest of honor. He asked what I did, and I said raise children.

"She reads more than anyone I've ever met," you added. You said you'd go get me a glass of wine. "And leave the high talk to the intellectuals."

Your friend laughed, because he thought it was banter. But I knew what you were saying.

OR

In the early weeks of a fetus's life, the heart occupies its middle. Then the heart moves high in the chest and down again. The stomach, the base of the throat: these places where the heart once beat remain the places

275

that feel. I remember when they throbbed for you. When we first met, I'd follow you on streets and stare at the back of your head, memorizing the flesh ridge of your ears, the curl to your hair. But the ghost hearts go quiet after so many years. You can forget they even existed, as I suppose you do.

The other day, he and I passed a woodpile. "Listen," he said, and held up a finger. "A woodpecker. Sounds different back home."

Together, we made the cartoon sound. I'd never do something that silly with you.

"Quiz me," he said last week. I'd been trying to choose the paint colors for the children's rooms. I held out the splattered hem of my shirt. Green, blue, yellow. He got each one right.

"In a year," he said, "I won't know the difference."

I told him something I'd learned once. The great impressionists had diseased eyes. "They only put a canvas at risk," he said. He knew that sounded bitter, so he added that maybe he should take up painting.

"Tell you what," I said. "I'll take up ballet. And then I can be your subject."

But now it's the weekend. You're back. And on the surface, things are fine, even good. The girls clamber up and down the stairs. The baby follows on his hands and knees. Everyone chases rabbits. We barbecue in the courtyard. You tell me that you love the gold wallpaper for the dining room. I update you on the roof. I tell you about the tile for the second-floor bathroom. I walk the line between faking and lying. I ask about your week, and the instant your mouth opens to reply, my mind is out the door.

"Super," you say. It's the same word in English and not the same word at all.

We sit outside and have a drink in the pergola. We talk about our dream house. Is that not what you called it when I first brought you here that summer when it still held renters, and we stood in the drive? Dream house, which translates into both languages? But what did I dream of, those years ago? I don't even remember.

What is your father like? he asks me. What about your mother? Do you have a middle name? Stop, he said once when I was in a patch of sunlight. Is that a scar? I laughed. "How can you see that?" And he said, "Because your arm is so close and always right next to me." So I told him about falling off my scooter when I was seven. I know you know the story, but I don't think you see the scar anymore, like a patch of ruched velvet over my elbow. Then I showed him the other scar, below my left shoulder. I told him how my mother used to tell me that our family had suffering in our blood, and that was why I became sick.

"So I'm going blind because there's something I can't see?" he said.

You've told me often that what my mother said didn't make sense. Why did it sound more true when he said it?

When I close my eyes as we make love, I'm looking at his face. As we fall asleep, that's his back, not yours, against mine. But at breakfast, I smile at you over the table. I hand you the baby. I say yes, let's go for a bike ride. There is nothing lonelier than being lonely with someone else.

AND

Another dinner at the cottage. It's raining, so my children eat with us. You're quiet across the table. You missed a spot shaving, on the edge of your jaw. Why didn't your wife tell you? She's taken my baby on her lap so that I can eat and is feeding him pieces of baguette. I get up to help the children cut their meat, because I can't sit here any longer. I don't want to pretend anymore. Until I met you, I thought I'd only have the walls to stare back at me, as blank and solid as everything I can't say. Like: Have I made a mistake? And: Is this it? A heap of ivy pulled from a bush. A strip of molding and a floorboard sample. A child's mouth opening to take in food. Small hands in my hair and large hands on my breasts.

"How is the work on the house going?" you ask me during dessert, in French this time, so to the table, and I say, *"Plutôt bien."*

"The wallpaper is up in the entryway," my husband says. "It's perfect." He smiles at me, and here comes the guilt.

On my way to the bathroom, I pass you as you leave the kitchen. The knuckles of your hand graze the knuckles of mine.

"Sorry," you whisper. "It's dark."

Upstairs in the bathroom, I close my eyes and put my forehead to the mirror. Out the door, you're gone, but there is the hall that leads to your bedroom. I stand in the doorway. One of those pillows is yours. Every night, you pull back those covers.

"Wrong turn," I say when your wife comes up behind me.

"It's that way," she says, and then, "I'm used to guiding people to the right place." She tries to laugh, and I realize I've only imagined she knows. And what is there to know anyway?

You are my husband, I remind myself the next day. I'm in the life we've built and it's a good one. You fix problems he never could: there you go to the phone to tell the contractor that the bill for the roof is wrong. "I'll go pick up a pizza from the truck on the square. You look tired. Don't cook." Goodbye, goodbye! I'll see you later. Down in the kitchen, I draw with the girls at the table. The painters have moved on to the trim of the third floor. The floor of the parlor has returned to a checkerboard, and the soot has been cleaned from the fireplace mantel. We'll sit by the fire during the winter. We'll host parties like they do. We'll get wrinkled together. I'll be content. Who wouldn't want this? If I were walking a railroad track and a train came from nowhere, you'd throw me aside and take its weight.

Later, as night falls, we sit in the pergola, facing the forest. You hold my hand and I lean my head on your shoulder. Anyone looking at us would think we are perfect, and I suppose that we are.

Let me tell you how I see the forest now, after having seen it during my childhood as a jumble of trees. Those branches that snake between the leaves resemble the veins and arteries that pull blood to and from the heart. All of life depends on such passages. Think of my breasts a year ago, when I was nursing. Milk through ducts. Footpaths through trees. The eye, too, is fed by a network of vessels, but his eyes have grown unnecessary roots. They swell and burst, creating a bulge that he sees as a dark spot in the center of his sight. His peripheral vision remains perfect, so when I walk at his side, he can see me.

Before we came outside to sit together, I put the girls to bed with *Le Petit Prince.* Do you remember what he says when he meets the fox?

"It is only with the heart that one can see rightly; what is essential is invisible to the eye."

And

How much is magic and how much is magic tricks? I keep thinking that if I look in the hat, I'll find the trapdoor to the rabbit. Every gesture, every word out of your mouth, has become a clue to a mystery that I might have invented. Today, when I meet you at the pond, you're skipping rocks.

"Try it," you say. "You look lucky today."

What does that mean? Later, as we walk a trail, your arm presses into mine. Was that an accident? A hand on my back over a stretch of moss. Careful, don't slip. When I'm the one who should be guiding you.

I let you see what you see, though I know I'm seeing what you can't. Details: the curl to a leaf, a trout that flips out of the pond. Pine needles flow over our heads. You tell me about a conference you'll go to next month.

"I can't operate anymore," you say, "but I can talk about operating."

Then you mention that you might write a book on a technique you invented. You could go into the heart softly, with needles, not knives. I say you should. You can't have my body but take my opinions.

"I'm catching it," I tell you when I see the toad. It leaps ahead into the camouflage of fallen leaves. I put it in your hands.

"Funny," you say. "It feels like a heart."

"Your fingers don't ever quiver," I tell you.

"Years of training," you say.

Then the backs of your hands in my palms, telling me, Open. That cold ball of flesh that trembles with fear, unsure where it has come to.

AND

Here's what could happen: Tomorrow afternoon when the children are with the nanny

282

and I'm supposed to be driving to Paris for
a chandelier, I come to your cottage. We lie
in that bed. I kiss your eyes and your chin
and your cheeks and your ears and your
neck. Your steady hands hold my back.

OR

Here's what could happen. I don't tell you.

AND

Or I tell him.

OR, AND

Then what?

AND

It's time, he says, to reciprocate your wife's
dinner invitations. I make deviled eggs. I
make meatloaf. All of this food that I don't
want to eat. I feel that I could never eat
again. The sound of the door knocker stops
my breath, but I continue to set the table.
The girls drag on my legs: "Mommy,
Mommy." Your wife gives them chocolates
wrapped in cellophane, which they rip open
and eat cross-legged right there on the floor.
Despite all the commotion, I'm quiet inside.
I pour you a drink.

"You look nice," you say.

My house and my children melt away, and

then reform when the baby cries. In moments like this, when I pick him up and he grabs my hair, my compass shifts back to its center.

He suggests a tour of the manor. I watch you as he puts his hand around my waist. Your eyes flinch.

"She gets the credit for everything," he says. "She's done magic."

In the parlor, he points out the nesting dolls on the fireplace mantel, and the relief carved into the stone. "They look like butterflies," he says, "but in fact, they are silk moths. And those are mulberries, though they look like grapes." You move closer out of politeness, but I know that the pattern hides under a cloud that will grow thicker each year until it covers your world completely.

"Let's have the aperitif upstairs, on the balcony," I say. "That would be more festive."

I have the baby in my arms, and yes, I know what I'm doing when I ask him to get the drinks. You ask her, "Could you lend a hand? You know me and stairs."

This is the first time we are cruel together.

I leave you in the hall to put the baby in his crib. We climb the stairs, side by side. You find the handrail for yourself.

"It's not finished," I say when we get to the room.

"You'll get there," you say.

On the balcony, I stand in your peripheral vision, perfectly focused. You lean toward me, and I lean toward you, and our hearts line up to beat together. Inside the house, the baby is crying. My hands on your back are as steady as yours on mine. And all around us, there are nothing but trees.

ACKNOWLEDGMENTS

Thank you:

To my daughters, Margot Deguet Delury and Rose Deguet Delury, for their joy and encouragement and for being them.

To the rest of my family, John Patrick Delury, Cecilia Delury, Vince Jacobs, Jeongeun Park, Sean, Senna, and Hannah Park Delury, Pat and Mimi Kearns, and John Francis Delury. Thanks, too, to Anton Deguet and his family, Gilles Deguet and Françoise Valtrid, Joris Deguet and Marie-Claude Dupont, and to Camille and René Deguet, who first showed me the forest.

To Jean Garnett, for being a dream of an editor, and Reagan Arthur and the entire team at Little, Brown. I could not be luckier to have my book in these hands.

To James Magruder, Marion Winik, Jessica Anya Blau, Elizabeth Hazen, Elisabeth Dahl, Liam Callanan, Peter Grandbois,

Kathy Flann, Christine Grillo, and Stephen Dixon and Alice McDermott for reading and editing me.

To Kendra Kopelke, Stephen Matanle, Betsy Boyd, Emily Gray Tedrowe, Laura van den Berg, Madison Smartt Bell, Gabriel Brownstein, and Paul Yoon for their writerly support.

To the organizations that have helped my fiction along: The University of Baltimore, VCCA, the Johns Hopkins Writing Seminars, the Maryland State Arts Council, and to the editors who have taken such care with my stories, in particular Tom Jenks, Cara Blue Adams, Linda Swanson-Davies and Susan Burmeister-Brown, M.M.M. Hayes, and Jeanne Leiby.

To my wonderful agent, Samantha Shea, and Anne Borchardt and the entire Borchardt agency.

To Don Lee, who believed in this book and in me and was with us every word of the way.

ABOUT THE AUTHOR

Jane Delury's fiction has appeared in *The Southern Review, The Yale Review, Narrative,* and *Glimmer Train.* She has received an O. Henry Prize and holds master's degrees from the University of Grenoble, France, and the Johns Hopkins Writing Seminars. She teaches at the University of Baltimore.

The employees of Thorndike Press hope you have enjoyed this Large Print book. All our Thorndike, Wheeler, and Kennebec Large Print titles are designed for easy reading, and all our books are made to last. Other Thorndike Press Large Print books are available at your library, through selected bookstores, or directly from us.

For information about titles, please call:
  (800) 223-1244

or visit our website at:
  gale.com/thorndike

To share your comments, please write:
Publisher
Thorndike Press
10 Water St., Suite 310
Waterville, ME 04901